Crystals, Belladonna, and Murder

Silver Circle Cat Rescue Mysteries
Book 1

Leanne Leeds

Crystals, Belladonna, and Murder
Silver Circle Cat Rescue Mysteries #1
ISBN: 978-1-950505-77-7

Published by Badchen Publishing
14125 W State Highway 29
Suite B-203 119
Liberty Hill, TX 78642 USA

For Marilyn

Of all God's creatures, there is only one that cannot be made slave of the leash. That one is the cat. If man could be crossed with the cat it would improve the man, but it would deteriorate the cat.

— Mark Twain

Contents

Chapter One

THE YOUNG GIRL COULDN'T SEEM TO DECIDE. I could see the frustration on her face, her eyes bouncing back and forth between the fluffy black and white tuxedo-colored kitten I'd been calling Pounce, and the regal-looking Siamese my daughter Evie had named Mister Me—because everything in his world seemed about him.

"I can't pick just one," she said.

"You have to pick one," her mother said.

"But I don't want to," the girl said. "They should have friends."

While the young lady's instincts were right in her desire to provide friendship for whichever cat she took home, the little female kitten and the snotty Siamese male with his nose in the air weren't exactly a match of destiny waiting to happen. She was looking for a playmate, while he was looking for a fancy couch to be displayed upon so he could be admired.

"Would those two get along?" the mother asked with a sigh.

I tilted my head and rocked my hand slightly in answer and then knelt down next to the little girl. "We'd let you take both of them home," I said. "But they probably need to go to separate homes, so they each get the attention they need. How about if I find another cat for Mister Me to play with? Or someone that's closer to Pounce's age and energy level?"

The little girl looked up at me, her eyes welling with tears.

"I know it's hard," I continued. "But you have to be strong and make a tough decision. You can't take every cat we have in here home with you, and you want to make sure the two cats you take home get along and will be lifelong friends, right?"

She nodded.

"You wouldn't want them to be unhappy or fight all the time, would you?"

She shook her head.

"So, which cat do you think would like your home better? Mister Me, who just likes to sit around and survey his domain, or Pounce, who likes to—"

"Pounce!" The girl's face lit up with a huge smile.

"Okay, Pounce it is," I said, scooping up the fluffy, long-haired kitten. "Follow me. I think I might have just the solution."

The girl and her mother followed me eagerly as we made our way to the back of the shelter, where cats needing a break from public display were housed. As we approached the non-public cat rooms, I could already see Pounce's tail wagging with excitement.

"You know who we're going to see, don't you, Pouncers?" I asked, opening up one of the doors.

"Who? Who?" the little girl asked.

Inside was another long-haired black and white kitten—Swoop—who was every bit as energetic and playful as Pounce. As soon as I put Pounce on the floor, the two kittens immediately ran over to each other and played together like they'd known each other forever.

The little girl watched them in delight, her face radiating joy. "They play so well together!" she exclaimed. "I think they like each other a lot!"

"They should," I smiled. "The vet said they're siblings. They were found together under a porch in Wagon Wheel Subdivision, and the owner of the house brought them in. They don't need to be adopted together, but I certainly think that would be a nice thing for them, and their new owners."

The girl nodded eagerly and crouched down on the floor next to them. She reached out her hand slowly toward them, as if she was afraid they might bite her or run off. But as soon as they sensed her presence, they stopped playing, turned toward her, and purred loudly.

"I think they like you," I said with a chuckle. "Go

ahead and pet them for a while if you like. They love attention. The other one's name is Swoop."

"Swoop!" the little girl squealed, clapping her hands excitedly. "He looks just like Pounce! Can we take them both home, Mommy?" The little girl begged, her eyes wide with pleading.

The girl's mother knelt down next to her and put her arm around her. "It looks like you've found your new kittens," she said with a smile, and then looked up at me. "We'll take them both home. If that's all right."

I nodded.

The little girl looked up at her mother with wide eyes. "Really?" she asked.

"Yes. I think it would be good for all of us to have a couple of new friends around the house."

The little girl grinned and turned back to the kittens, who were now tangled together in play. "Thank you, Mom!" she said, throwing her arms around her mother's neck in a hug.

I couldn't have been more thrilled as the woman handed over the paperwork and the adoption fee. It was always gratifying when we could find suitable homes for our cats, but it was especially gratifying when we could find homes for siblings together.

I knew these two kittens would have a lot of fun together and give each other—and this excited little girl —a lifetime of love.

"I told you we should have had Pounce and Swoop on display on the public adoption room," my daughter said as she finished the adoption paperwork for the two kittens. "Hey, Mom, can you hand me my..." Evie frowned. Then she point toward a Yeti tumbler at the other end of the counter. "Hand me my..." She jabbed toward the tumbler more insistently.

"Your drink?" I asked, grabbing the metal container.

She nodded and took the tumbler I held out to her. "The two of them were like matching salt and pepper shakers."

"I didn't always put them out alone," I told her.

"You should never have put them out alone. I'm just saying."

A soft, almost imperceptible mewing came from the cubby to the right of the reception desk, and when I leaned over to check, a tiny kitten looked up at me with tiny wet eyes.

"What's the matter, baby?" I asked, walking over to investigate.

He was trying to stop his body from shaking. When he heard the cage door open, he turned and scrambled to the opposite side, as far from the opening as he could get.

"Hello, there." He stared at me. "Are you having a problem?" I asked the tiny black and white cat. His little head bobbed back and forth as he meowed. "Are you hurt, buddy? Hungry? Thirsty? Bored? What's wrong?"

He cocked his head to the side and stared at me, his ears alert, and pointed forward.

"What's wrong with him?" Evette asked from nearby.

"I don't know. He wasn't jittery like this yesterday." I squatted down to get a better look.

He was a small cat with big, green eyes and a patch of white fur adorned his chest, a ghost mark in a sea of solid gray. The interior of the cubby looked clean, but it smelled like someone had missed the last litter box cleaning. Maybe let it get a little too full.

"Hello, baby," Evette said in her high-pitched, singsong voice crouching a few feet away. Her small hand approached the cat, her palm open. Her eyes never left the cat, who looked at her out of the corner of his eye, but he made no move to attack. When she was close enough, the cat immediately pressed his head up against her hand and let out a long, low wail.

"Oh, baby, what's wrong?" Evette cooed. "Are you hurt?"

"I already asked." I know that sounds ridiculous, but unless you've had a cat, you wouldn't understand that. "The only thing I can see is the litter box is a little ripe," I told her, pointing. "Maybe he just wants it cleaned."

Evette leaned toward the cage, her hand out flat, inviting the kitten to climb in. "Why don't you come here? I'll get you out of there and get that clean for you."

The kitten's cries ceased, and he tilted his head to the side as he studied her. His eyes dilated to large, impossibly green ovals as he took in her form, assessing whether she was friend or foe.

Evie held her hand still, but didn't force him to jump down. "Come on now."

The cat sniffed, his nose twitching.

"You can do it. Come on."

The little black and white cat sniffed at her once more, his whiskers close enough to tickle her skin. He then padded toward her hand and stopped just before her wrist. The baby cat's eyes seemed to bore into her as he prepared to pounce. But instead of biting her, he licked her wrist.

"Aw, you're a sweetie!" Evie said, picking him up and cuddling him close. I could hear the contented purr as she cradled him in her arms and walked him to a clean enclosure on the other side of the room.

"Mrs. Rockwell?"

Ugh. That damn title.

Despite being divorced for years, people continued to refer to me as Mrs. Rockwell, as if I was still married and hadn't moved on from my past years ago.

I hated how that Mrs. title made me feel: small, insignificant. Permanently attached to a man I couldn't stand. It seemed like no matter how hard I tried to shake it off and be seen as my own person, people just couldn't seem to let go of the idea that I was still some kind of relic from a previous life—

"Mrs. Rockwell?" The tone was more insistent.

Oy. Drifted off for a minute there. I looked up. "Yes?"

"There's a phone call," Darla Montgomery, a

college-aged volunteer at the shelter, called from the front office. "It's some Deputy Markham from the Tablerock Police. Or the county? I'm not quite clear. He said he needed to talk to you."

Lots of people weren't totally clear.

Texas was a unique place in a lot of ways.

So, each of Texas' 254 counties elected one sheriff for their county—Sheriff Bob Dixon was ours. He managed our county's fifty deputies in nine satellite offices and one large county jail. Sheriffs and their deputies are county-wide peace officers with the authority to act in both unincorporated and incorporated areas of a county.

So, anywhere and everywhere.

In the county, at least.

Tablerock, being a town, was incorporated, and Deputy Markham's satellite office within the tiny police headquarters allowed him to monitor the goings on in Tablerock and report back to the county anything they needed to know.

"Hey, Eleanor," a gruff, friendly voice said from the other end of the line. "This is Deputy Markham. Do you have room for an older cat today?"

"Hello, Deputy, how are you?" I said. My voice sounded friendly, but I was annoyed at the question—of course, we had room. We always had room. And if we didn't have room, we would make room. "Yes, certainly."

I paused, waiting for Deputy Markham to continue, but he didn't.

"Deputy, is there something else? I'm just curious because you usually just come by. Is there anything particular that led you to call me about it instead of just bringing the cat over? Something we need to prepare?"

"Well, he's a little older than most of your cats, and I think he's had a rough time." There was an awkward silence on the line, filled weirdly with uncertainty and hesitation. Finally, he spoke once more. "Look, Eleanor —it's Fiona Blackwell's cat, Belladonna. We just arrested Fiona for the murder of her husband. Beau Blackwell didn't leave her as she claimed. They found him dead in a ditch in Burnett County."

"Fiona Blackwell's cat is female," I informed him.

"Okay, she is older."

I blinked as I processed the rest of what the detective said. "Murder! That's terrible," I said, as if I had a clue what Fiona Blackwell would claim about her elderly husband. Which I didn't. Well, not really. "That seems crazy. I mean, that woman must be almost a hundred years old!"

"Not quite, but close. Anyway, Fiona's pretty insistent the cat needs to go to you and that I need to bring this...drink tray with her. Or a table top. Maybe it's a litter box? I don't know, it's this big circle thing. Looks like a drink tray from a casino to me."

"A drink tray?" I blinked. "The cat needs a cocktail tray?"

"Yes, ma'am. Old Fiona Blackwell may be one bubble off a plumb, but even her crazy is pretty insistent. She says if that tray doesn't go with that cat, that cat may very well rip the throat out of anyone that comes near her. Fiona says you'll know what to do with it."

"Oh, Deputy, I doubt that. On all counts."

"I don't doubt it about the throat-ripping. This is a pretty pissed off cat."

My curiosity was eclipsed by worry for Belladonna. "Bring her over. We'll take care of her."

I heard the deputy audibly sigh with relief. "Thank you, Eleanor. Look, I know Fiona—that is to say, she knows me—and I know she's not entirely...normal." I wish he wouldn't, but in small town Texas, that word still had meaning. "But the woman is over eighty, and she damn near adores that cat. I'd like to follow her wishes if I can. Give her one less thing to be upset about. Maybe she'll confess if she knows we're taking care of her cat. You know what I mean? Save us all heaps of trouble."

"I understand, Deputy."

"I'll be over in a few. Thanks, Eleanor," Deputy Markham said, and then he hung up.

"What was that about?" Evie asked me.

As I hung up the phone, I delivered the news to my daughter. "Fiona Blackwell was arrested for murdering her husband," I said.

Darla's footsteps thundered through the house as she ran to join us. The disbelief was clear in her shocked expression. "Murdered?" she gasped.

I nodded. "Detective Markham has her cat, and Fiona was insistent the cat—and a cocktail tray, if you can believe it—have to go here, to Silver Circle Rescue."

"Belladonna's coming here?" Evie asked me.

Darla's eyebrow lifted in a haughty arc as she said, "To be fair, it's not like she was going to go anywhere else. The county shelter is a joke, and Fiona would have gone on a hunger strike before letting her precious Belladonna spend a night there." She glanced at Evie before continuing. "I'll check JuxtaPorte. You check SocialBook?"

Evie nodded.

The girls pulled out their phones, their fingers skimming over the screens with practiced ease. They found the social apps with the juiciest town gossip threads and eagerly tapped them open. Their eyes scanned the posts impatiently, looking for something interesting. When they found something, they announced 'facts' as they discovered them, their voices laced with excitement.

"She was arrested about three hours ago," Evie said, her eyes scanning.

"The police busted down her door," Darla whispered. "Oh, that poor woman."

"Poor woman?" Evie looked up. "They're accusing her of killing her ninety-year-old husband."

"Accusation is not guilt, Evie," Darla disagreed.

"She's been telling everyone in town that people in suits and hats were watching her," Evie said, waving her phone around wildly. "And that her husband was fine. He was just on a trip, and he was coming back from the North Pole, where he'd been abducted by a group of aliens who wanted to take him to their home world." She held up her hands. "Can we at least agree she was nuts?"

"You just read all that?" I asked, pointing.

Evie nodded.

"We can agree she was in her eighties. That's all I'm giving you right now," Darla said. "I would think you, of all people, would withhold judgment on something like that."

My daughter's lips set in a firm line. "What's that supposed to mean? Me, of all people?" Evie asked, her expression incredulous and visibly annoyed. "I didn't kill anyone. She was arrested for killing her husband—I have nothing in common with her."

Darla looked confused. "I didn't mean anything like that. I just mean with your—"

"Okay, let's not, ladies," I said, jumping before she mentioned something that would infuriate my daughter. "What I want to know is this: how does an eighty-year-old woman get a body to the next county over? And then dump it? Mr. Blackwell wasn't exactly a small man, and Fiona is pretty tiny," I said, leaning against the counter. "Does she even drive?"

Evie shrugged. "I don't know."

"I do. I know she doesn't." Darla crossed her arms.

"She can barely walk across the street without having to stop to rest, too."

"How do you know that?" I asked.

"I follow her on JuxtaPorte, and I cat-sat for Belladonna last year when the Blackwells went on that Thanksgiving trip," she said with a shrug. "And before you ask, no, I have nothing better to do with my time."

"Clearly," Evie muttered.

"She couldn't have done it," Darla said. "She just couldn't have."

"Do you know anything about this drink tray the deputy is bringing with her?" Darla's head tilted slightly as she shook it from side to side. "Okay, then—the cat is coming soon, so we need to get the isolation room set up. Let's let the gossip drop and get to it so Belladonna has a safe space, poor thing," I said, trying to change the subject.

I knew better than to talk sense into either of them when it came to gossip. They would both be like sharks with blood in the water, circling and waiting to take a bite out of the next juicy piece.

"Sorry, ma'am," Darla said.

"Yeah, sorry, Mom."

The girls nodded in agreement and then walked toward the isolation room while continuing to scroll aimlessly through their phones.

It was a wonder neither walked straight into a wall.

The gossipy posts about Fiona Blackwell and the

murder of her husband, Beau, apparently had the town of Tablerock in a frenzy of speculation.

Fiona Blackwell, a murderer. It was shocking.

I pulled out my phone and scrolled. Fiona Blackwell, who had always been so proper and put-together, was now the center of a media circus. Photos of her being led away in handcuffs splashed across my news feed, and the town's SocialBook was alive with speculation about why the old woman murdered Beau Blackwell. Speculative posts were marked by a flurry of comments, likes, and shares as the townsfolk tried to make sense of the scandal.

Chapter Two

THE DELIVERY DOORBELL RANG, AND I RACED TO answer it. "Who is it?"

"Deputy Don Markham." The deputy's voice was clipped and precise, conveying a sense of urgency and command, and was sprinkled with just a bit of exasperation. "I have Belladonna with me."

Right. Not a cat person.

I wiped the sweat from my brow, swung the door wide, and motioned for the deputy to enter. "Come in, sit down. Let's just get Belladonna settled, and then you can get back to your work." The deputy looked weary, as if he had been battling a great adversary. "Well, shoot. You look like you've been through the wringer. Are you all right?"

"Ellie, I don't know how you and your girls do this every day," he said, in a familiar, yet still professional, tone as he shook his head in disbelief. "I feel like I'm dealing with a psychotic toddler. Give me dogs any day. You just tell them what to do, and they do it." The deputy thrust the cat carrier forward. "Cats are not right in the head. They're just not."

"Of course she's right, Deputy Markham," I said. "Cats are unique creatures, and they're always perfect just the way they are. Belladonna," I said. "Come here, sweetheart." I opened the carrier door and held my hand out. She leaned into it and allowed me to stroke her behind her ears.

"You can just keep the carrier. It belongs to the cat. She will not come out."

As if she heard the deputy, a cat with a lustrous black coat and bright, piercing eyes, walked out of the carrier and hopped into my lap, curling her tail gracefully around her paws. Belladonna's ears lay flat against her head, and her tail quivered gently from side to side as she regarded the deputy with distant curiosity.

"You can't be serious," he said to the cat.

The cat purred low and rhythmic, almost like a deep hum, as her lithe muscles rippled under her smooth coat.

"I spent two hours trying to get her into that damn carrier, and she just wouldn't budge from behind the bookshelf in Fiona's house. Oh, she's a beauty, all right," the deputy said. "But she's also an untamable beast." He placed a stack of paper on top of the carrier. "Good luck with her."

In response, the cat's hiss was deep, loud, and angry, and she scurried back into the carrier.

I rolled my eyes.

Dog people.

"She's just a cat, Don. You've just taken her from her home and placed her in a new environment that smells like other cats she's never met before. I suspect you smell like dogs—the ones you have at home and the ones at the station. Belladonna has every right to be concerned."

Markham shook his head as he pointed to the cat. "You may need to take the top off that carrier. Once she hisses, all bets are off," the deputy warned me.

"She'll be fine." I moved the carrier down to the floor (far away from the anti-feline detective) and opened the door as wide as it would open. Belladonna immediately stepped out into the room and rubbed against my leg. "There you are, sweetie." I smiled as the cat sat daintily next to me. She moved with an elegant grace, meticulously grooming herself as she surveyed her new surroundings.

"That cat hates me." Belladonna glared once again at the deputy, as if daring him to comment once more. Deputy Markham glared at the feline. "She did that just to spite me."

"Oh, for goodness' sake, Don, she did not," I told him, dropping his title and switching to the more familiar first name. Belladonna purred as I scratched her head. "What a good girl you are," I crooned. "Don't listen to him."

Looking frustrated and slightly beaten, Don Markham let out a heavy sigh. "Sure. Fine. I'm glad someone thinks so, because I sure don't. That cat is nothing but trouble. She scratched me when I tried to put her in the car. Through the cage." He rubbed his arm ruefully. "I don't know what Mayor Fiona was thinking about that crazy animal."

I looked up. "Mayor Fiona? Is that some weird nickname?"

"No, ma'am." The deputy gave a dismissive wave of his hand. "Fiona was the mayor of Tablerock. About twenty years back, maybe? Honestly, I'm surprised you didn't know that."

How would I know that?

I only moved here five years ago.

"I did not know. I would never think she used to be an elected leader, considering the way she barks at everyone and makes up crazy stories. And the way the entire town seems to think she's insane." It was strange to think Tablerock once elected someone so abrasive and difficult to get along with. "At least judging by the SocialBook posts."

The deputy shrugged. "After the Blackwell scandal, they voted her out of office. Well, to be more accurate, the city council forcibly removed her. Councilman Hammond made a speech about how dirty politics have become that the town could turn on her like that, but they kicked her out, anyway." The deputy shook his head in disappointment. "I think all that infighting was terrible for the city. I genuinely think Miss Fiona got a raw deal."

My eyebrows shot up. "The Blackwell scandal? Isn't her name Blackwell?"

The deputy sighed and leaned on a cat tree. "It was a long time ago—

"I know. Twenty years. You said."

He looked at me with an eyebrow raised. "Yes, but everyone still talks about it. It was just before Fiona lost the election. Her husband, Beau, the recently deceased? They caught him cheating on her with some other woman, and it caused quite a stir in town."

"Oh?" I always wondered who this mysterious "they" was, and how "they" always seemed to be in the right place at the right time to know everything important that no one else would know but for "them."

"Well, it wasn't just some other woman," Don said, amending his gossip as he shifted away from the cat tree to lean against the wall and put his elbow on the cat tree. "It was with Jessa Winthrop. She was serving for Place three on the city council. It was a pretty big scandal because they were all in government. It devastated Fiona, of course."

Of course.

The deputy kept going. "And the whole town turned on her. They said she must have known what her husband was doing, and that she was just as guilty as he was."

I blinked.

That took a turn I wasn't expecting.

"No one would believe her when she said she did

not know. Jessa and Beau were both voted out of their positions on the city council, and Fiona lost the mayoral election shortly thereafter."

"Why would it matter?" I frowned. "Whether Fiona knew or didn't know, she didn't do it. He did. Why on earth would the town blame her for her husband's cheating? That makes no sense."

The deputy shrugged. "I guess that's just the way it goes sometimes. People can be pretty ruthless with scandals like that, especially in a small town. No one wants to be associated with someone who's been in one, even if they were in it through no fault of their own." He sighed and shook his head. "It was a real shame—but the real benefit went to Jessa Winthrop, weird enough. She ran for mayor in the next election and won in a landslide. She's been our mayor ever since."

I loved this town, but even I have to admit it could be a little weird.

"You're a young guy, Deputy." I said as I scratched Belladonna's head. Don Markham was around thirty-five years old—young for a silver-haired, almost fifty-year-old like me. "How do you know so much about the town's gossip from twenty years ago?"

Don Markham's face pinked with embarrassment, his eyes downcast as he fidgeted. Then there was a half-smile. "My mother, ma'am."

"I see," I said. Then something nagged at me about what he'd said. "Wait a sec. Don, can you just clarify something for me?"

He nodded.

"Are you saying that Jessa Winthrop is the mayor because Fiona's husband—who Fiona just supposedly killed—cheated on her years ago?"

He nodded again.

"That seems awfully far-fetched."

He shrugged. "I don't know how to explain it, but that's what happened. My mom said people saw Jessa as the more sympathetic character in the situation. They perceived Fiona as cold and heartless because she did not publicly break down when her husband cheated, didn't go after Jessa, nothing. Jessa, on the other hand, was viewed as a victim of Beau Blackwell's manipulation because she was constantly crying. At least, that's what my mother said at dinner last night when I mentioned the case."

Could it be that simple?

Fiona remained stoic, Jessa wept openly, and so the entire town sided with the emotional woman over the stoic one that had been wronged in every sense of the word?

I doubted it was that simple, but this was a small Texas town.

Maybe it was that simple.

And that was ridiculous.

"I always see Fiona walking around town with a scowl on her face, and she has nothing nice to say to anyone. Maybe there's a reason she's been a sourpuss since my daughter and I moved here," I said. I reached down and scratched Belladonna once more. "Even knowing all this, Don, I still can't believe a woman of her age murdered her husband."

"They may have been legally married, but Beau and Fiona hadn't lived under the same roof for twenty years," the deputy said. "Oh, before I forget. Here's the cocktail tray thing. Fiona didn't say why it had to go with the cat, but she was insistent I bring it here, too. Maybe it's Belladonna's food bowl or something?"

I wasn't interested in the silver dinner tray, Deputy Don's twenty-year-old gossip, Mayor Jessa Winthrop's philandering, or Fiona and Beau Blackwell's bizarre—and now fatal—marriage. I was too preoccupied with my own thoughts and responsibilities to care about the sordid past of two geriatric (and one post-geriatric) people I barely knew.

I placed the tray on the ground and watched Belladonna sniff around it, her tail twitching with delight. She then placed her front paws on the plate's edge. Her bottom wiggled left to right, her tail thumping rhythmically on the ground. The thumping was punctuated by a high-pitched squeak.

I laughed out loud. "What are you doing, silly cat?" I asked, reaching down to pet her.

That was the moment I saw it.

A seam that wrapped around the metal plate's

outside lip, occupying at least a quarter of its circumference. I felt along the seam and found a small lever on the tray's outer rim. When I pressed it, a hidden compartment opened.

"Well. This is interesting."

Inside, there was a stack of yellow papers and a faded photograph. I picked up the photograph and gazed at it for a moment, mesmerized by its age and delicacy. Setting it down, I reached out and gingerly picked up what appeared to be newspaper articles. The old paper was brittle in my hands and tore as I tilted it back and forth to read some headlines.

CAT SPEAKS AT OLDS TOWN FAIR

TRAVELING PSYCHIC MAKES ANIMALS TALK

PSYCHIC DOOLITTLE WOMAN MAKES PETS SPEAK

"What is that?" Evie asked as she came into the isolation intake room. "Is that the silver tray Fiona said we had to take with the cat?" I nodded. "Do we know why yet?"

"Look at this. It was in the tray." I gave Evie the old, yellowed papers I pulled out of the secret compartment. They were so fragile, and I was afraid I would tear them. "Be careful." She plopped down on the chair as Belladonna stepped over to her, purring. "What do you make of that?"

"Huh. Did you see the picture?" Evie reached down to pet the cat as it rubbed against her leg. She fixed her gaze on the papers in her hand, and I could see the gears in her head turning as she read. She frowned again as she looked at the paper. "The top of the table looks a little like the cocktail tray thing." She looked up. "Maybe it's not a drink tray at all."

The lady in the photograph was older than me, but not as old as Fiona. She had the same sour expression as Fiona Blackwell, though. She appeared to stand in front of a small table, with a huge white cat perched on top. There were three other cats in the picture, two on the floor and one in a chair next to the woman. All were haughty as they looked into the camera.

"Maybe she was a clairvoyant?" Evie asked. "Something like that, anyway."

"A clairvoyant?" I repeated. "You mean like that guy on TV that claims he can talk to the dead?"

She laughed. "No, that's a medium. I mean like with animals. Animal communication is telepathy, actually. I think she would talk to the animal and then tell the owner what it had said." Evie carefully held out one article. "That's what this one seems to say."

I rolled my eyes. "Oh, come on. People are so gullible. They were gullible then. They're gullible now." I touched the crystaline inlay. "It is lovely, though."

"Some people believe in that kind of stuff. I mean, I believe a little. That's possible, at least," Evie said with a shrug. "And if this woman could actually do it—"

"Oh, come on. Sweetie, you can't be serious."

"People would surely line up to speak to their pets and find out what they think, right?"

I shook my head in disbelief. "Oh, Evie. People don't listen to their pets now," I said, frowning.

Evie looked at me, one eyebrow raised. "Cynical much?"

Yes, okay.

That wasn't entirely true.

Running an animal shelter, though, it was easy for me to become jaded. I saw too many animals neglected, or worse, and it was hard to remain optimistic in the face of that.

Many people loved their pets, and they would probably pay handsomely to know what was going on in their furry friend's head. That means anyone with a knack for theatrics could convince people—

"Do you think Belladonna is trying to tell us something?" Evie asked me, glancing down at the cat now curled up in her lap. One paw extended far out and lazily tapped against the rim of the silver circle, leaning against the chair, as if she was trying to get its attention. Belladonna's yellow eyes stared up at Evie, unblinking. "That's kind of weird, right?"

I shrugged. "Maybe she just misses Fiona. Maybe the cat's just attached to the antique, and that's why Fiona sent it over." I frowned. "Had it sent over." I looked up at Evie. "I can't believe a woman that old is in the county jail. I mean, that's just awful."

We both fell silent, lost in our own thoughts.

I thought about the gossip Markham told me about Fiona Blackwell, and I wondered what really happened —twenty years ago and last night. If Don was right and the two hadn't lived together for twenty years, why would she up and kill him now? I mean, wouldn't killing Beau twenty years ago be more...well, understandable?

"Let me see those one more time," I said, and Evie handed me the papers. I stared once again. "It really looks like that drink tray, doesn't it? On the table? Such a strange history."

The mystery woman in the newspaper articles was dressed in a flowing skirt, and she was holding a deck of cards. It was obviously some kind of performance. It couldn't be Fiona Blackwell...

Well...

The articles were from the forties. That was eighty years ago.

Fiona's mother, maybe?

I lowered my gaze to the silver platter.

It glinted in the light, its smooth surface reflecting the sunlight pouring in through the window like a mirror. The scalloped edges and raised circles and half-moons on the edge gave the thing a delicate, intricate appearance. At the center of the platter was inlaid crystal with an almost ethereal glow, like glass infused with luminescent crystals.

It could be a large metal platter, a drink tray, or a round shield. It could be a circled mirror that had the glass replaced with whatever that inlay was made of.

One thing was for absolutely certain; I didn't know what it was or why it had to come with Belladonna, and Fiona hadn't sent instructions.

Glancing at Evie, I shrugged and put the papers back in the compartment. "I have no idea what this thing is, but I need to get back to work. It's almost eleven, and I want to finish up the paperwork for Belladonna before lunch." I reached down to pet Belladonna, and she licked my hand. "Can you help her acclimate?"

"Sure. No problem," Evie said, her gaze on Belladonna as the cat rapidly tapped her paws against the edge of the tray. Evie was fixated on the feline, her attention completely captivated by its movements.

Chapter Three

The following morning, Evette and I were working in the main house, which had the most kennels. We had to wake pretty early to clean the pens, empty the litter boxes, and do some general maintenance before the cat rescue volunteers showed up—or any adopters rang the bell looking to give someone a home forever.

"I'm running out to get the litter," I told Evie.

She nodded.

The sun was a sliver of light when we began work, the air heavy with silence and moisture. The dewdrops glinted like diamonds in the early light, making the yard seem enchanted. I could hear the buzzing of insects in the distance as I grabbed the bags of litter from the storage area, a siren from the main road breaking the silence.

Evie and I worked quickly, knowing that the day would grow warmer and busier as it wore on.

Even though it was January, we still lived in Central Texas. In our part of the Hill Country, north of Austin, the average high temperature in January was sixty-one degrees. (That's sixty-one degrees Fahrenheit for those of you who switched to the metric system to make things easier on yourselves.)

I knew it would be hot that day.

Texas was almost always hot.

Except when it was freezing.

The cats walked excitedly over the hardwood floors, recently polished. The tables and couches were arranged just so to give cats and humans ample room to sit and get to know one another on the plump and inviting furniture —free of cat hair for the moment. The walls were a clean slate gray so the cats would pop against the neutral walls. Every flat surface glowed with cleanliness.

We worked hard for that.

I walked by the front desk and stopped short, frowning. The curtains in my window partially blocked my view of the road leading to the house, but I could still see the flashing lights of the police car at the entrance to the shelter.

It didn't have its siren on, but...still.

I leaned forward and opened the window, trying to get a better look. The cruiser was idling at the edge of our property, its engine purring like an animal at rest, and the officer leaned against the car, his head turning slowly from side to side as he scanned the area for something.

Or someone.

I felt a prickle of unease and leaned closer to the window.

The gate to the shelter was about a hundred feet from my window, so I was close enough to see his hands moving rather oddly. I squinted, trying to see what the cop—and there was only one—was doing. Was he on his phone? He turned.

Yep. He was.

He was leaning against the car, talking on the phone.

Try as I might, I could not hear what he was saying, but his body language was tense and he kept looking around as if he was expecting someone.

I took a deep breath. Normally, I wouldn't worry about it too much, but with a murder fresh on everyone's minds and the murderer's cat in my shelter, I realized it might pay to be a little extra cautious. I approached the intercom system. Turning it on, I spoke into the microphone."Good morning, officer—can I help you?"

There was a crackle of static, and then a voice came through. "No, ma'am, Mrs. Rockwell."

I winced.

That 'missus' title again.

I never even lived here while I was married.

The honorific "missus" felt like a noose around my neck, and every time I heard it, it made me think of my failed marriage. It felt like a scarlet stamp that reminded me of my mistakes: the man I'd loved by mistake, and the betrayal I'd experienced.

Yes, I was a single divorced woman with a disabled adult child, but did that mean I had to have a permanent reminder of a broken past as part of my name? I should be able to move on with my life without constantly having to think about what happened.

"Are you sure, Officer—"

"Winthrop, ma'am. I'm just waiting for orders."

"Well, if we can help you at all or if you'd like some coffee, let me know."

"Yes, ma'am."

As if my intercom call had spooked Officer Winthrop, the officer scrambled back into his vehicle and pulled away as I watched from the window.

I guess those orders came in.

Rather convenient timing, those orders.

I turned back to the desk, and noticed my heart beating as if I had sprinted a mile or climbed a mountain or something. I could feel my pulse pounding in my neck. A slight noise from behind made me jump.

But when I turned around, there was nothing there.

Oh, Eleanor, get a grip, I told myself.

I've always been a little high-strung. Staring down the barrel at fifty, I suppose that wasn't about to change. I took a deep breath.

It was probably nothing.

Evette, my twenty-two-year-old daughter, walked out of the kitchen and glared at me. Her hand was planted on her hip, and her head tilted to the side. "We're out of coconut milk. Are you going by HEB today, or do I need to call an Uber to take me to Starbucks tomorrow morning for a proper coffee?" she said.

She followed that speech with a withering look.

"Heaven forbid," I said, pulling myself up to my full five feet, five inches. "Just add it to the list." I pointed toward the computer with my index finger. "You can use the regular milk for now. It's in the fridge." I tried to keep my voice light, but still saw a flash of sanctimonious disapproval cross Evette's face.

"I could. But I will not. I need my coffee to have the creamy, coconut goodness that only comes from non-exploitive creamers." She sipped her coffee, savoring the rich flavor. "I had enough for today, but tomorrow, I'll be super grumpy if I can't have my coffee." Her eyes pleaded with me as if her coffee addiction was a matter of life or death.

"Again, you can have your coffee with milk."

"Cow's milk is intended for baby cows, Mother."

"I understand you feel that way," I responded with respect. That switch to calling me mother was never a good sign. "It would just be—"

"I'm not taking away milk from a baby. That's insane."

I was 'Mom' when she took me for granted, or she felt a sudden swell of affection. I was 'mother' when she was annoyed and wanted to emphasize her displeasure.

I did not respond.

And when it was clear I would not respond, my daughter stared at me with a determined look, her eyes narrowing. "I need coffee with coconut milk, and let me explain once more why."

I could feel the tightness in my jaw as I fought the urge to point out there was no way any baby cow would drink the filtered milk in our fridge now or in the future —but my daughter's eyes were earnest as she spoke about her belief that cow's milk was unnatural for humans and how the dairy industry was cruel.

I tried to remember that she was coming from a place of compassion, but it was hard to see past the annoyance I felt at her repetitive preachiness. I took a deep breath and reminded myself that this was a weekly argument and that we always ended up in the same place. That if I reacted with annoyance to something she said, things would shift and be even worse than tolerating a lecture from my know-it-all daughter.

She was an adult—legally, at least—but her disability left her in a nearly perpetual state of irresponsibility. She had too many challenges to be self-sufficient, and I was the person left to pick up that slack. I wanted her to be self-sufficient at some point, and I was supportive of her attempt to break free from all the parental strings wrapped around her because of her disability.

I was trying to let her unwind them one by one.

Trying.

It wasn't easy.

The doctors in Houston told me it was a miracle she made it through the surgery. Her heart had been so weak, and she'd been through so much. I stayed by her side the whole time she was there, but it was hard. Seeing her hooked up to all those machines, barely hanging on.

It was the hardest thing I ever went through.

And it was the third time I'd done it.

And, by the way, the third time I'd done it alone.

When we finally got to come home, she was...different.

She was quieter and more withdrawn. She had trouble remembering words, even favorite colors and foods, and could not seem to hold some thoughts from one moment to the next.

What was even worse? She realized she was different. Once that sunk in, Evie didn't want to do anything but sit in her room and read to escape the gloom that took over. It was like the light had gone out in her life.

My girl, who had once been so free and carefree, and who delighted in trying new things, now became someone who needed a routine to steady her. The stability of the familiar grounded her when her brain started to...have issues. It grounded her when her mind...hitched.

That was what we called it.

Hitched.

"You know how important my coffee is to me."

The pleading in Evie's eyes was all too familiar. I knew that look. It was the same look she gave me when she was five and wanted to stay up past her bedtime. Or when she was ten and begged for a dog. I knew I was supposed to say no. I was supposed to be the bad guy sometimes.

But after everything Evie had been through, was having the creamer she preferred really so much to ask?

"I'll run over to the HEB in a few hours," I told her. She looked relieved. "Thanks, Mom."

Oh, good. I was Mom again.

I finished the paperwork from the day before and called Belladonna's veterinarian to make sure she had all the shots she needed to be released from isolation. Despite the upheaval in the cat's life, Evie reported she appeared somewhat content, so I didn't see why we should keep her in isolation for too long.

We avoided using kennels and I hoped I'd be able to do that with Belladonna—despite Don's warning the cat was like a hell-cat on paws.

I wanted her to play with a toy mouse and smell the fake pine tree, meet the other cats, and just be a cat again. It seemed like the least we could do for her after everything she had been through.

The antique grandfather clock in the front foyer told me it was already noon.

Noon. Where did the day go?

I quickly tidied up the front desk, locked the front door, and flipped the sign, telling folks we would be back in an hour. Once Darla knew I'd closed the shelter for lunch, I headed to the isolation room (stopping by the fridge to grab a ham and cheese sandwich.)

Evie sat at the table, looking annoyed. A cup of coffee and a half-eaten sandwich sat next to her laptop, which was open in front of her.

"Hey there," I said, hoping her coconut creamer annoyance had passed.

"Sorry," she mumbled, her eyes on the screen, "I got hungry. I wasn't sure how long you would be." She pushed the plate and cup aside and gestured for me to sit next to her. "I figured I'd eat here. I guess you had the same idea. I didn't want to leave Belladonna alone for too long this first full day."

"It's fine," I said. When I reached the table, I placed my Diet Pepsi next to her coffee and then sat down. "How is she doing?"

Evie shrugged as she took a bite of her sandwich. "She seems fine, honestly." Her eyes darted around the room, and a smirk twisted her lips. "I put her water on that platter thing. I don't know what it's for or why we have it, but hopefully, it'll help Belladonna feel at home, I guess. I have not fed her yet. I want to make sure she doesn't throw up the water from stress."

I nodded, taking a sip of my soda. "So, what do you think is going on?" I asked Evie. I pointed toward her computer. "You find anything out?"

"With the murder or the platter thing?"

I held up my hands, palms out, as if to say 'one or the other.'

"Well, I can't find anything about that woman in the newspaper, but it all may just be too old, right? I can't find anything on that drink tray thing, either." Evie sighed and ran a hand through her hair. "So, I honestly have no idea."

"Do you think Fiona Blackwell is the woman in the articles?" I asked.

"No. That woman looked your age in the forties. Which was eighty years ago. So I don't see how it could be. She's been long dead, right?" Evie frowned and shook her head as I frowned and tried not to bite back at my daughter calling me old, though her observation was spot on.

"It could be her mother or grandmother. Or it could just be the person who owned this thing. Maybe she just bought it from an antique shop in Kerrville or Salado or something. She never noticed the secret button? I don't know."

Suddenly, a voice neither of us recognized joined the conversation.

"It's not her."

We looked at one another.

"Did you say that?" I asked.

Evie shook her head no. "You?"

"That wasn't me."

The voice was female, and deep, slow, and sultry. She had an almost European accent that sounded vaguely English.

"Down here."

Evie and I looked at one another, shock and disbelief on our faces. "Are you serious? It's not, right? It can't be."

"Of course not. It can't be," I agreed.

"You people really are slow, aren't you?" the voice said. There was a hint of amusement in it, a hint of irony.

Evie shouted, "Who's there? This isn't funny. Darla?"

"No."

We looked up.

"Wrong direction."

I couldn't believe that a human voice could come from somewhere other than a human mouth, so that was what I looked for. A person or a speaker or a radio. Even a phone propped up in a corner. I don't know why we looked everywhere but the place we knew the voice was probably coming from.

It's clearly human nature to avoid looking squarely at the obvious if the obvious makes absolutely no rational sense.

Eventually—finally—we both looked at the cat.

Belladonna sat with her legs curled underneath her

and her tail lazily draped over the edge of the silver platter. The platter's crystal center glowed with a golden radiance that would challenge the sun to a staring contest. The cat was as dark as the night, her eyes two intense golden orbs that glittered with sanctimonious amusement.

"Belladonna?" I whispered, not sure if I was seeing what I thought I was seeing.

Or hearing what I thought I was hearing.

"Did that cat just...talk?" Evie asked in a choked whisper.

The black cat stretched lazily, her body lengthening and her eyes growing wide and alert. She turned in a circle, her claws clicking against the tray like a metronome. Satisfied, she walked over to where we sat.

"It couldn't have," I said to my daughter and the cat.

She jumped into my lap and curled into a ball, rubbing her cheek against my hand, looking for a scratch or a rub behind the ears. The further away Belladonna got from the silver circle, the softer the illumination became, until the crystaline center was once again clear, colorless, and dim.

I scratched behind her ears, and she flopped onto her side.

"What is going on here?" I asked the cat.

Belladonna stared at me with an elegant yet unblinking and penetrating gaze.

Then she meowed.

It was a simple, normal meow—the meow any

domestic house cat might give in response to being scratched behind the ears. But somehow, coming from Belladonna, it sounded like a question.

"What's going on?" I repeated.

Evie looked at me, her eyes wide with wonder and fear. "This is crazy, right? I mean, cats can't talk."

No, they cannot.

Belladonna stretched again and hopped off my lap. She sauntered over to the silver tray and splayed out across it, her head pillowed on her paws. She stared at us, her eyes half-lidded and lazy, as the tray beneath her glowed once more.

Chapter Four

Evie furrowed her brow and tilted her head, clearly struggling to understand what had just happened. We locked eyes.

"I don't understand," I said. It was as if my mind was stuck in a loop, unable to come up with an answer.

"She's a cat," Evie said, as if it were obvious. "I mean, she is...right?"

"Everyone knows that cat," I said, my thoughts still racing. "Fiona's had her for as long as we've lived here. Her Pictogram is filled with pictures of the cat. So she's definitely a cat."

Evie's eyes widened, her mouth slightly ajar. "You follow Fiona Blackwell on Pictogram?" Evie asked.

"She submits pictures every year for the holiday calendar," I told her.

"I didn't think people your age even knew what a Pictogram was."

I let my gaze slide over to her, a look of annoyance clear on my face.

"What?" she asked. "Sorry."

I turned my attention to the cat. Belladonna sat quietly licking her right forepaw, her golden eyes fixed on it with the intensity of a race car driver passing someone on a new track. The cat looked up from her grooming and steadily returned my gaze.

"This is impossible," I said, staring at her. "Cats can't talk."

"Stellar point, Mom." Evie rolled her eyes.

The cat slowly rose to its feet, its fur sleek and black as midnight, paws padding softly against the ground as it stalked toward Evie.

With wary eyes, my daughter watched the cat intently.

Belladonna rubbed her head possessively against Evie's leg before looking up at her with those bright golden-yellow eyes. Her tail swished back and forth as if marking her claim.

Evie kneeled down, her eyes locked on the cat. "Look, cat," Evie told her, "I like you, but you're kind of creepy."

"Oh, she's not creepy," I said reflexively, my full-throated defense of felines and all their creepy, predatory behavior always at the ready—but I noticed my voice didn't sound confident. I looked down at Belladonna, her expression a mixture of fear and suspicion. "There must be an explanation."

Belladonna sneezed.

"Okay, sure. An explanation." Evie looked around and then pointed as we both sank back down on the chairs. "Maybe it was just the intercom misbehaving. A passing radio from the street. So, maybe you're right. I mean, she's not talking now, is she?"

"No, not that I can hear," I admitted.

Belladonna meowed in response and then hopped up onto the table. She plopped down between me and Evie and licked her paw lazily once more (pausing every so often to point an interested nose at one of our sandwiches.)

"Well, she's not saying anything anymore," Evie said, taking a big bite of her sandwich. "So, that's that, right?" She looked at me, her brow knitted in concern.

Belladonna stretched out her front legs, lowered herself down, her head resting on her paws. She closed her eyes and a soft rumble emanated from her.

I watched Belladonna intently.

Evie eyed her carefully as she chewed, as if waiting for her to speak.

"Well, I mean, she's vocalizing. Like a cat. The way cats do," my daughter clarified haltingly, her eyes glued to the black cat lying across the small table.

"And yet we both heard something," I muttered.

"Yep. We both heard it."

Belladonna lazily opened her eyes and looked up at me, the gleaming intelligence and unreadable expression causing a jolt of unease. She cocked her head to one side, watching me with curiosity, and loudly meowed.

"Yes, you can meow," I said. "Very nice, sweetie."

The cat meowed again, this time in a more impatient tone.

"What are you trying to say?"

She meowed once more, her feline tone strong and imperious as she jumped down from the table and sauntered over to the platter. Belladonna walked with purpose, her movements graceful and regal, as if she were the queen of the house. With steady steps, she made her way to the silver circle at the center of the room.

The platter suddenly flared a bright yellow-gold, and the cat asked, "Canst you comprehend me, cretins? Need I lower my breeding to putrify your primitive capacity for intellect?" Belladonna's voice was low-pitched and sharp, like the hiss of a serpent or the roaring of a jaguar, and filled with an air of arrogant confidence.

Well. That was rude.

I looked at Evie, and she returned my gaze with wide eyes.

"Okay, this is getting weird," she whispered. "Mom, you're seeing this, right? I'm not having one of my mini-strokes? I'm not hallucinating? The brain damage hasn't bothered me a lot lately, but now I'm wondering."

"I'm not sure what's going on here, but I think we're

both seeing and hearing the same things. You're not having a stroke, honey," I told her.

The cat's eyes were firmly fixed on us, her head tilted slightly to the side as she surveyed us with a perplexed expression.

I swallowed. "So you can talk. What else can you do?" I asked, fearing this was only the beginning of whatever Alice in Wonderland experience my daughter and I appeared to be having.

There was a low, rumbling purr that slowly built in intensity as she moved, her paws padding softly against the smooth surface of the platter. The bright yellow inlay continued to glow warmly with each circling motion. "My capabilities are far from limited, as you can clearly see.," she said.

"Oh?"

The yellow glow contrasted with the cat's sleek black fur, turning her lithe form into a dazzling display of shifting shadows and warm golden light. "It is not a question I think applicable to our current discourse," the cat told me smugly.

Though...to be honest, I couldn't be certain the cat was saying it.

Belladonna's mouth made no visible movement. The words appeared almost bodiless, as if they were coming from a PA system in the room that made the sound appear to come from everywhere. The platter's golden light pulsed with each word, like a speaker that reacted to music's beat.

I stared at the circle platter drink tray thing.

"I see you've figured it out," the cat said, now with a pleased expression. "Fiona told me that you could easily be reasoned with, since you are well mannered and blessed with intelligence. Without sharp wits, one could not hope to corral this many felines."

"Did she?" I whispered.

Belladonna let out an airy sigh as she settled back down on the platter. Her long, slender body relaxed and her paw gently traced over her glossy fur as she groomed herself idly once again. "You are a human, and I don't know if I can ever trust you entirely after the destruction that has ensued due to your species. We were a peaceful, natural society before humans came here. You hurt each other, and you hurt animals," she said matter-of-factly. She stopped licking and looked up. "Despite all that, Fiona said I could count on you. That I could trust you."

I could feel my pulse pounding in my temples as I struggled to maintain an expression of calm and nonchalance.

I had little interaction with Fiona Blackwell since I moved to Tablerock five years ago, and what little interaction I had with her wasn't all that great—she screamed at me at the grocery store once for taking up the entire aisle with my ample backside. (Okay, she didn't say ample backside. Her vocabulary was much more robust.)

"Trust me for what?"

"Assist my endeavor to release Fiona from her cage,

as I should like to be getting home," Belladonna said (as if it should be obvious.)

"Like, solve the case of who really killed Beau because she didn't?" Evie asked, "Or, like, break her out of—"

"The former, obviously." Belladonna sneezed. "The latter, if necessary. Obviously."

Obviously.

"And if they send her away to the penitentiary, you'll need to provide me a good home—one that serves me a gourmet diet at least three times a day, and gets plenty of sunlight each morning—but doesn't expect me to simply watch the outside through a window."

Evie smirked, the corners of her lips lifting as she let out a low, quiet chuckle. "Anything else?"

"And there will be no dogs." The cat looked at my daughter expectantly and her whiskers trembled slightly. "None. Not here. Not anywhere I go. Speaking of other things I want—I believe it's past lunch time, and despite your concern for my constitution, I guarantee you I am not that delicate. Get me a bowl of your finest." She sniffed. "Even though it will be far beneath what I'm used to."

"Please?" I hinted.

"Yes, thank you," Belladonna responded.

"Do we call Deputy Markham?" I asked as we watched the cat tear into a bowl of soft food through the observation window.

"And tell him what?" Evie responded. "That we have a cat that can talk?"

"Well. Yes. That Fiona Blackwell's cat can talk," I replied.

She shook her head. "I think we're better off keeping this to ourselves for the moment."

"Why?"

"Well, for one, because we have a talking cat and a magic platter, and I, for one, need time to process the realities of that," Evie said. "Two, because I'm not sure we can trust him."

"What?" I asked, a slight frown creasing her forehead. "What do you mean?"

"I mean, he's Deputy Markham. He's the one who arrested Fiona."

"But—" I froze and looked down the hallway.

Darla leaned out, smiled, and waved.

Evie and I waved back.

Darla disappeared into the main room.

I frowned and lowered my voice. "You said we can always trust the county over the city because the city's kind of a two-horse town with nepotism running amok, right? And he's with the county."

"I know what I said, and I meant it, but again—he's the one who arrested her and he's the one who has her in jail," Evie pointed out. "I don't think we can trust him."

"I guess I can see your point."

I couldn't. Not really.

She looked away from the glass and sighed. "I don't know what to do."

"I still think we should bring this whole thing to Deputy Markham," I said, my eyes still fixed on the black cat. "I mean, we have to tell someone."

"Unless..."

I looked at her. "Unless what?"

Evie's gaze shifted away from the glass, and her eyes met mine. There was a hint of uncertainty in her expression, as if she was conflicted about something. "Unless we just do it."

"Do what?" I furrowed my brow in bewilderment. Sometimes Evie loses the thread of truth in what she's saying, but I didn't sense that was happening here.

"What the cat said."

My mouth opened slightly. "I'm not breaking an eighty-year-old woman out of jail, Evette," I said. "Are you out of your mind?"

"I don't mean that. I just mean we can't just let someone accused of killing their husband rot in jail just because the police refuse to investigate other suspects."

"How do you even know that's what's happening?"

Evie pointed. "The cat. Obviously."

Why did everyone think everything was obvious?

I turned away from my daughter, my chest tightening as a piercing ache settled in my stomach. It was hard, sometimes, to know when she was talking clearly or just off on an odd brain-hitch tangent. "I don't think anything is as obvious as you think it is, Evie. What do you want to do here?"

"We figure out who really killed Beau. Then Fiona gets out of jail, Belladonna goes home to her, Fiona takes back the weird magic platter, and none of it's our problem anymore." Evie held her hands out. "It's a win-win. We don't have to tell anyone a cat told us. We protect their secret and solve the case."

Not a tangent, then.

I frowned. "I don't know."

"I don't know, either, to be perfectly honest," Evie said, her voice wavering slightly. "I'm still not fully convinced I'm not having a stroke."

"If you have to ask, you're probably not."

"But I know one thing—if that is a magic platter that lets people talk to cats, Fiona sent it over here and risked us knowing her secret to get our help. Well, your help." She shook her head, a slight flush coloring her cheeks. "No one in this town really notices me."

"Evie—"

"Actually, you're right."

I didn't say anything.

"That's just my brain telling me things." She shrugged again, looking down at her hands. "Fiona noticed me. She's always been nice to me. She's never been mean to me, and she always stopped to talk to me when we saw her in the store—and she talked to me like I was a person, not like some disabled, heart-diseased, brain-damaged, one-foot-in-the-grave person. You know?"

I knew.

I remembered.

But I also knew the long-standing rumors about Beau and Fiona, how they despised each other. I hadn't been in town that long, but I'd been around long enough to hear that. Just because a cat told me her eighty-year-old owner was innocent didn't mean she was innocent.

But I said none of that to Evie.

I nodded. "Okay, I understand your sense of obligation here," I said. "I do. But we are not detectives. We're not police. There's only so much we can do here."

"I think we have to do something," Evie said. "Maybe both things."

I had no idea what two things were.

"We figure out who really killed Beau, and we help Fiona and Belladonna."

Oh.

Those two things.

Evie and I stood at the isolation room window in silence for a long moment, our eyes fixed on the obnoxiously smug cat as it tore into its food.

Finally, I sighed and turned to my daughter.

"Okay," I said. "As long as you understand that this might not be as easy as you think it's going to be."

"I know," Evie said. "But we have to try."

No, we didn't.

We really didn't.

"For now we'll keep the talking plate between us, and as long as we take it slow, and we're careful there's probably no harm is seeing what we can find out," I said. "But carefully. I don't want either of us getting hurt."

Evie nodded vigorously. "Of course not," she said. "We'll be careful. I promise."

I hesitated for a moment longer, then finally nodded. "All right," I said. "Let's do this."

Why did I agree?

Well, because I was an idiot, that's why.

I wasn't a detective. I didn't know how to investigate a crime. I had no idea how to discover who had killed Beau, and I had no idea how to help Fiona. I sure as hell didn't know what I was supposed to do with a talking cat.

I sighed and rubbed my temples, trying to calm down.

Laurie, my best friend, was always telling me my biggest issue was that I couldn't say no to my daughter. That I needed to learn how. That I needed to stop putting my life and my needs on the back burner for the sake of Evie.

I'd never really paid much attention to that before, but now I was beginning to understand what she meant.

Maybe Laurie was right.

That inability to say no usually involved something

simple like charging the newest cell phone to my overused credit card even though I couldn't afford it, or an ill-advised trip to Disney World when I had to borrow from my IRA to pay for the expensive hotel with the animals off the balcony.

This was no trip to Disney World, though.

Even I could see that.

It was—possibly—a matter of life and death.

Fiona was in jail, and while I didn't know what she had been charged with, it was enough to get an eighty-year-old woman put in jail with no chance of bail.

Probably premeditated murder.

That would mean she planned and killed her husband.

I thought about what Evie said about Fiona, how nice that old woman had always been to her. How she had always treated her like a person and not like some invalid. It was hard to reconcile that with the rumors swirling around town for years, rumors that Fiona and her husband hated each other. Rumors he was cruel, and she was crazy.

Ugh.

I didn't want to be involved in this.

But I couldn't say no to my daughter, and I doubted I'd ever be able to.

Since I hadn't said no, I needed to find out what I had just got us into.

"Evie," I said once Belladonna was satisfied with our lunch service, "I need you to take care of the shelter while I'm gone."

"Okay. Where are you going?" she asked.

"To see Fiona Blackwell."

Obviously.

Evie nodded. "That's probably a good idea." Her smile was weak and cautious, a nervous expression in the face of uncertainty. "Darla and I will hold down the fort here until you get back," she said.

"Good deal." I grabbed my keys."

Behind me, she called out, "Be safe."

Chapter Five

TABLEROCK'S A SMALL TOWN BY BIG CITY
standards, but a decent-sized town by small town standards. It had quaint houses and well-manicured lawns lining its streets and a few larger buildings nestled along the main county road. The jail sat at the very edge of town, a small brick building with heavy metal doors and barred windows.

A quick phone call to Deputy Markham when I was on my way, however, confirmed Fiona's detention was at the Wildebridge County Jail.

"Why are you going to see Fiona Blackwell?" he asked.

"Thanks! Oops, have to go. I'll talk to you later!" I responded and hung up. I didn't want to lie to Don, but I certainly wasn't going to tell him the truth.

That left awkward avoidance.

My thoughts wandered as I negotiated the curvy

country roads that led from Tablerock to Woodville, Wildebridge's county seat. The twenty-minute drive was one I'd driven many times, and my attention split between navigation and the talking cat back at Silver Circle Cat Rescue.

Maybe the cat wasn't really a cat, I thought.

My grandmother, rest her soul, had been an enthusiastic patron of the supernatural. She would tell me whispered stories when I was a child about fairies, leprechauns, and mermaids. Creatures just out of sight, but ones that could also be seen if you knew how to look for them. It used to drive my mother crazy, that my grandmother insisted magic could exist for me if I believed hard enough.

"Believing," she'd whisper with a knowing smile, "is what makes the magic real, Ellie. You remember that, now."

I remembered.

But I never believed it.

Driving to the jail, though, I questioned my grown-up dismissal of her convictions, wondering if there was any truth to her words.

What if Belladonna was proof of the existence of magic? If she could speak, then...well, what else was plausible? Perhaps leprechauns and fairies existed in some version of reality. Maybe my idealistic grandmother was right all along. She swore they—magical creatures—could be seen clearly if one was only patient and observant.

I was not patient, and I was definitely not observant.

I was so lost in my own thoughts, I almost missed the sign for the jail turnoff. I jerked the wheel and veered onto the road, my heart racing as I took in the imposing structure ahead. The large parking lot and four-story cinder-block building were covered in bars, their darkened windows like pools of ink. The parking lot was filled with cars and was ringed by rows of menacing-looking barbed wire fencing, as if daring anyone to attempt an escape.

It was a grim, dismal place.

A metal sign, small and dark with the faded word 'Visitor' etched across its face, hung crookedly from a post cemented into the asphalt. As I turned off the ignition and stepped out of the car, I could practically feel the building's ominous atmosphere reach out for me. It just felt...lonely.

Isolated.

Sad.

I pressed the black buzzer set onto a faded golden plate beside the large doors. A voice crackled through the intercom, asking who I was and why I had come. Once I gave my name and told them I was there to visit Fiona Blackwell, they buzzed me in.

So far, so good.

The sharp chemical stench of bleach flooded the air, causing my eyes to water and my nose to sting. I felt sneezing and coughing coming on as I weaved through the crowded room, my gaze fixed on the guard with the metal detector wand hanging loosely from his hand under the visitation sign.

"Fiona Blackwell?" I asked him.

He ignored me.

A television, perched next to the guard's desk, featured a brightly colored game show that blared loudly, drowning out my voice.

"Excuse me, I'm here to see Fiona Blackwell?" I asked again. This time my voice reverberated even more loudly than the obnoxious game show.

The guard barely glanced at me as he waved me through without searching my belongings, waving the wand over me, or even looking away from the screen.

I could have slunk in with a gun and he would not have noticed.

Which was not exactly a comforting thought.

Anxiety made my stomach turn and my heart beat faster.

Once I was through the checkpoint, I made my way down a dimly lit hallway, the rubber soles of my sneakers making a squeaking sound. As I turned right at the end, I was greeted by a hulking brute of a man. A thick neck sprouted from his shoulders like an oak tree and bulging arms the size of tree trunks hung from his body. I felt a mixture of fear and determination as I approached him.

And "greeted" was a generous word.

"What do you want?" he asked, his voice gruff.

I scanned his badge—C.O. Max Reynolds. Max's badge glinted in the overhead fluorescent lights, his uniform crisp and pressed, his stance rigid with concentration. He appeared almost robotic as his eyes scanned my body, searching for any hint of danger.

"Yes, I'm here to see Fiona Blackwell," I said.

"Do you have ID?"

I exhaled slowly, feeling my stomach knot with anxiety. I really, really didn't enjoy being out of my element, and this place was far from my element. I showed Correction Officer Hulk-Smash my driver's license, and he pulled it from my hand and ran it through some machine. After a few moments, he handed it back and said, "You can go on back. Visiting hours are from 9 a.m. to 3 p.m. You can't stay over thirty minutes after you start, and have until 4:00 to leave. You understand?"

I nodded.

He raised his eyebrows.

"Yes, sir," I answered.

He looked at me for a moment, then slowly reached for the buzzer to let me in.

I smiled.

He didn't.

I said thank you.

He grunted.

I continued down the long and narrow hallway lined with doors leading off in various directions, all unmarked. The harsh fluorescent lights flickered and buzzed like the ambient lighting in a horror movie.

Suddenly, I came to a large room.

To the right were a collection of tables bolted to the

floor and the wall. Each table contained an antique-looking phone with a large, round handset and rotary dial in front of a large, scratched-up rectangle of glass. The walls were a dingy gray, washed out by the harsh lights above.

Cheerful.

Upon seeing me, a female guard, Leila Tucker, pointed toward the tables. "Thirty minutes from when her ass hits the chair, and not a minute more. You hear?"

"Yes, ma'am."

I sat at an open table and took up the receiver. Over the intercom, a disgruntled voice asked me the name of the inmate I wanted to see, as well as my name and relationship with the requested inmate. I introduced myself to the guard as a friend (lacking a better explanation regarding why I was there) of Fiona Blackwell.

There was a click and then silence.

Leila, meanwhile, chatted on her cell phone about her boyfriend, a Tablerock police officer. "Ever since his brother showed up, he's been crazy. I just wish this was over already, you know? I mean, I get it, but enough already."

The movement of Fiona Blackwell's shuffling footsteps, the guard's firm grip on her arm, and the clinking of the shackles around her wrists I heard through the wall showed the weight of the old woman's predicament. Her face looked strained and haggard, her skin worn and tired. She seemed so small and vulnerable in the orange jumpsuit, dwarfed by the guard who escorted her. She looked nothing like a cold-blooded murderer.

I noticed the old woman's eyes were sharp, though, as they bored into mine.

The guard uncuffed one of Fiona's hands and attached her to a metal loop on the prisoner's side of the table. Fiona's face, set in a hard, stony expression, studied me carefully. Her neck pulsed in time with her rapid heartbeat, the only indication of anxiety or unease.

I pointed to the phone on her side of the glass.

After a pause, she reluctantly picked up.

"Hi," I said, feeling awkward.

She said nothing.

I cleared my throat and tried again. "How are you?"

Fiona's fingers curled tightly around the receiver, her knuckles white and her grip unwavering. Her expression remained impassive.

Okay, then.

I swallowed hard and continued on, trying to ignore the pit that formed in my stomach as I spoke with this strange and (supposedly) dangerous woman.

"I'm not sure if you know who I am. Or remember me. My name is Eleanor Rockwell. Ellie for short. I mean, you can call me Ellie," I said nervously, the setting and Fiona's stare making me more nervous than I'd been on my first day of high school. "They dropped your cat, Belladonna, off at my shelter. Silver Circle Cat Rescue?" I paused. "Because you told them to?" I paused again, waiting for her to acknowledge she knew who I was.

When that didn't happen, I cleared my throat and asked politely, "Ma'am, did you hit your head or anything when they arrested you?"

Fiona finally spoke, her voice soft and raspy. "You don't need to say anything, honey. I know why you're here. I also know you probably won't believe me when I say I'm innocent because of all the rumors about me floating around this town."

"I don't know of any—"

"Don't lie to me. I won't lie to you. But I am innocent. I did nothing wrong." Fiona paused and took a deep breath before continuing. "I know this whole thing looks bad. But I can explain everything."

"Ma'am, I'm not a lawyer," I said with a placating smile. "I'm not here about Beau. I just want to know what's going on with that drink tray thing you had Deputy Markham bring to my shelter." She glared at me. "The one brought in with your cat?" I leaned in as her eyes narrowed. "It seems like," I lowered my voice to a whisper, "the cat can talk to us when she stands on it."

Fiona's eyes darted back and forth, scanning the room for signs of danger or intrusion. "Keep your voice down!" she said through clenched teeth. Her eyes became small and hard. "Maybe you're not as smart as I thought. Since you came here from Austin, I thought you might be a little more on the ball than these country yokels, but I can see the obvious flies right by you sometimes."

Well.

Ouch.

The old woman's expression was guarded and watchful, as if trying to remain inconspicuous. "Did you ask Belladonna why I sent them to you?" she asked me.

"Did I..." I trailed off, puzzled, and furrowed my brow. "I'm sorry, did I what?"

"I think everyone in this town is a boneheaded fathead," she said with a sneer. "Did Belladonna tell you I didn't kill Beau, at least? Even though that cheating jerk was so crooked he had to unscrew his britches at night? Britches he'd take off for anyone other than his wife!" Her eyes blazed with anger and betrayal as she spat out the furious words.

"Ma'am," I said, trying to break in, but Fiona kept going. "Mrs. Blackwell—"

"I sent that cat to you because I need your help," Fiona said, her eyes glinting with a seething rage. "You're the only one who can clear my name. You're the only one that would listen to a cat, so you're the only one who can help me get the actual killer caught."

"Me?" I asked, shocked. "You want me to interrogate a cat? Ma'am, I—"

"No, I want you to help me catch the actual killer. Look, I didn't kill Beau," Fiona said. "And I'll get a lawyer and do my best to convince the courts in the normal way, but Belladonna knows more about Beau and me than anyone else." She glared at me, daring me to disbelieve her. "That cat is almost twenty years old. I got her when Beau left me for that born-sorry, mean-as-amama-wasp, uppity Jessa Winthrop." The old woman leaned forward aggressively and whacked the scratched glass between us. "Belladonna knows all of it."

"Knows all of what?"

Fiona's piercing gaze was fixed on me, her lips pressed into a thin line. "I can't say anything here." She held the old-fashioned phone receiver in front of her, waving it back and forth at me like it was a weapon. "The walls have ears."

But we can talk about a talking cat?

"Okay, ma'am." I took a deep breath. "I'm trying to understand what you specifically want me to do with Belladonna and the magic platter. Do you want me to take your cat and the platter to your lawyer so the cat can give him information?" I asked, still confused.

Fiona's face was a mask of disbelief. "You're not seriously suggesting this, are you?" she hissed. "If word got out about the talking cat and platter, they would be taken away for sure! Government experiments, the Mafia, Russian spies...who would believe us? Only those people would, and they'd all come for that circle. And my cat! But the deputy?" She cackled. "They would laugh us out of town, or worse. No, it's too dangerous. We can't take that risk."

I sat there for a moment, trying to take it all in.

If anyone overheard her babbling about her cat, the star witness in whatever plot she had to clear her name, they would think she was deeply troubled, perhaps unhinged or even insane. Tossing up the Mafia and spies stealing her cat was...it made her sound crazy.

But I knew that cat could talk.

As crazy as her rapid, rambling words were, I wasn't sure Fiona Blackwell was wrong.

Fiona sat anxiously on the edge of her chair, her hand gripped tightly around the receiver as she stared at me with wide eyes. She appeared a little desperate, actually. Her expression was tight with worry as she furrowed her brow in concern.

I sighed. "Okay. Again—what specifically do you want me to do?"

Fiona leaned forward. "I need you to keep my Bella safe. That is the first. But I also need you to help me solve Beau's murder and clear my name. Once we catch the actual murderer, they'll have to let me go then!"

She was repeating herself, and she'd told me nothing about the crystal plate.

Then again, giving me the weird plate's background probably was not her top priority at the moment.

I sat in silence, feeling torn. None of this—her arrest, her husband's death—had anything to do with me. At all.

But I'd seen the cat talk with my own eyes.

Well, I heard it with my own ears.

If Fiona was telling the truth—and she was an innocent woman—the cat might be the only living thing on the planet that knew how to prove it. Since I was the crazy cat lady, maybe she figured I was one of the few people that would be more concerned for Bella's safety than for the magical platter.

At least, I thought that was why she sent her to me. Maybe.

"Okay," I said finally. "I'll try to help you."

Fiona nodded gently, a look of relief etched on her features. "Thank you," she whispered. "I knew I could count on you. We're good people, you and I. Cat people. We cat people... Well, we cat people have to stick together." She glanced at the clock. "Our time is almost up. Next time you visit, I'll tell you all about the platter."

Little did I know Fiona Blackwell would be as dead as the husband they accused her of murdering before we had the chance to talk again.

The faint whiff of fresh blossoms and herbs greeted me as I pushed open the door and stepped into the cool, dimly lit back foyer. The scents of catnip and lavender were soothing, evoking a sense of safety and comfort. The air was heavy with the familiar aroma, and I relaxed a little.

"It's about time you got home," said Evie, walking in. She set the box of litter on the hallway counter. "How was it?"

"Sorry it took so long," I said. "How's Belladonna?"

The isolation room door creaked as Evie pushed it open, and I winced at the sound, half expecting

Belladonna to come flying out at me like she was aware of my first refusal to help her owner. But the mysterious cat was in the room, as expected, asleep on the silver platter, her chest rising and falling slowly with each breath.

I snuck a hand toward the cat's head, carefully avoiding startling her. With my other hand, I petted her head lightly in small circles. "You poor baby," I whispered.

Belladonna's eyes flew open, and she hissed at me. A snarling voice echoed off the walls of the small room. "Back off, human—"

I quickly pulled my hand away and stepped back, half expecting her to jump off the platter and attack me.

"—before I tear your throat from your—oh," Belladonna said, the tone suddenly calm. "It's you." She looked at me for a moment, as if trying to decide whether to trust me. Then she slowly lifted her head and stretched it toward my hand, which I extended back to her. Belladonna sniffed. "That is a truly awful scent. Did you swim in a vat of bleach?"

I carefully stroked the black fur between the cat's ears. "I did not, no."

Her whiskers curled against my fingers as she closed her eyes. The cat tilted her head back, exposing her throat in a show of trust. "That smell is truly horrific, but that feels good," she told me. "Don't you dare pick me up, though."

"I won't. I won't hurt you."

"I do not make the same commitment to either of you." Bella's rumbling purr vibrated through her feline body as her eyes slid shut once more and she nestled into my palm. Then one eye popped open. "As if you could hurt me," the black cat sniffed haughtily. "I am a mighty hunter, despite my years."

"You didn't answer. How did it go?" Evie asked again anxiously.

"Fine," I replied. "Weird. I'll tell you in a bit." I glanced back toward Darla in the next room with a prospective adopter and then back down at the cat at the center of it all. "You didn't tell Darla about the platter, did you?" I asked.

"No. Why?"

"I think the fewer people that know, the better," I told her. "We don't want to tell anyone else until we can sort through what's going on."

"I promise not to tell a soul," Belladonna said in a rumbling purr.

I stroked the cat one last time before pulling my hand away and leaving the isolation room with Evie. Things were about to get very interesting indeed.

Chapter Six

"ALL THE CATS ARE FINE. WORK IS DONE. STOP doing, start sitting, and tell me what happened." Evie sat on the couch, watching the moonlight play on the floor. She held a cup of steaming tea, the sweet berry aroma wafting to fog up her glasses. "And I don't want the five-minute whispered version. I want to know everything."

I told Evie about my visit to the jail, not leaving out any details. I told her about the frosty air and the echo of my footsteps down the linoleum corridors. I described Fiona's thin, angular face, her wide eyes, and her wacky assertions. The way she would look at me like she was figuring something out and then look away. I could see the gears turning in Evie's head as she processed the information. "Honestly, I'd say that old woman was completely bonkers—and guilty—if I hadn't heard the cat talk myself," I admitted.

"Bonkers, okay—but guilty? Anyway, you know, I'm not sure she's wrong," Evie said when I had finished.

"About the Mafia?"

My daughter's eyes rolled and her face pinched with a young person's impatience. "I could see that thing being dangerous if it was in the wrong hands. In fact," she said, getting up carefully off the couch to grab her laptop, "I bet someone tried to take the platter from her mother, and that's why they disappeared."

"I'm not following. Who disappeared?" I asked her.

She clicked her mouse and pointed to the faded words on the screen, her face set in a grim expression as she read through the details of Abigail Wardwell's mysterious disappearance. "Abigail Wardwell, mother of Fiona Wardwell, who is now Fiona Blackwell—and Mom, since we're the Rockwells, I have to admit all these well names are making me raise my eyebrow, too."

"Why?"

"I don't know. Because it seems weird?"

I leaned forward and squinted.

She displayed an old article about the disappearance of Abigail Wardwell from Fort Worth after B.L. —Barnaby Lafayette—Hunt, a swarthy Texas oilman, tried to buy her "talking disk." "According to this, there were rumors Hunt stole the platter and killed Abigail after she refused to sell it to him, but no one ever followed up on the story. Or if they did, they didn't print it."

"Huh," I said. Belladonna looked at me and sharpened her claws on the scratching post. "That's strange."

"That's not even the half of it," Evie said as she pointed to the image of H. L. Hunt with an expression of disgust. "Dude was a bigamist. He married multiple women and had fifteen children. I mean, just based on that, I'd say this guy was not one to take no for an answer with grace. He definitely didn't think the rules applied to him." Her expression was intense and determined, as if she were searching for answers hidden for years. "Anyway, Mrs. Blackwell—Fiona—probably has reason to be a little paranoid about what people would do to get the thing. I'm a little paranoid after reading this."

Evie gave me an uneasy smile and looked down at her hands. Her long nails dug into the red fabric of the sofa, and I waited for her to say something more, but she appeared done with her observations.

"I agree," I said. I reached up and gently tucked a stray lock of hair behind her ear, eliciting a smile from her. "But I don't think it's like a Marvel movie where suddenly its existence is going to cause the Age of Ultron or whatever. I agree we can't let anyone else know about it, but I don't think we need to order a bunker just yet."

Her shoulders loosened, and she nodded. "Yeah, okay. This stays between us," she said, her face serious. "For now, at least. What should we do with it? We can't just leave it sitting here."

A sleek and muscular tuxedo cat named Sylvester

flexed his lithe frame as he moved, his large, piercing eyes gleaming in anticipation as he stalked toward one of the food bowls. His glossy black coat was accented by bold white markings along his face and paws and a dashing white bow tie.

"What do you need, Sylvester?" Evie asked.

The cat meowed loudly, a clear sign of hunger and impatience.

"You'd think he didn't just have dinner an hour ago," Evie chuckled, and then turned toward me. "What do you think?"

"I don't know," I said, glancing at the screen and thinking. "I think we need to come up with a list of questions for Belladonna first. And we can only talk to her at night when everyone's gone home. I can go see Deputy Markham tomorrow and see if I can get any more information from him that might help us, get a sense of why he arrested Fiona."

"And me?"

"You need to pull every article anyone's written on Fiona and Beau and find out what their deal is."

She nodded slowly, a look of relief washing over her face as she realized that we finally had a semblance of a plan.

"How are we so calm about all this?" I asked my daughter.

"I don't know, Mom," Evie said. Her eyes were bright and alert, her expression calm and composed.

"We've just dealt with a lot in our life, I guess, so we're good at rolling with the weirdest punches."

"That we are," I agreed.

My daughter smiled then, her eyes lighting up to make her look almost childlike. "I don't know that a magic platter is any weirder than a tiny zapper in my chest making my heart beat, right?" she said, referencing her pacemaker—a modern miracle she depended on for survival.

"You're right. If you told someone a hundred years ago that you had a tiny machine in your chest that made your heart beat properly, they'd think that was magic," I said, smiling back as one of the recent orange rescue kittens batted at a belled feather on the floor. "I guess this is just the next level of weird."

"You've got that right," she said, her eyes crinkling in amusement. She hugged me tightly. "I love you, Mom."

"I love you, too. And I'm so proud of you."

"For what?" she asked, furrowing her brow.

"For being you." I smiled. "But mostly for not letting your anxiety overwhelm you when a talking cat shows up in our shelter."

Evie rolled her eyes slowly in annoyance and let out a sigh. She was unimpressed by the compliment. "Okay, so we will gather information, and tomorrow night, will we talk to Belladonna?"

"I think that's best. No idea, really, what happened with Belladonna, what she saw, or what she knows. I don't want to traumatize the cat by peppering her with questions we could have found out another way."

Evie nodded. "Sounds good. I'm going to dig for a bit more on the net and then go to bed." She sighed as she righted herself, her long legs unfolding from underneath her as she pushed herself up from the couch. With her laptop before her, she stepped slowly toward the door. With a final "Night, Mom," she returned to her room.

I stayed in the main room of the shelter longer, surrounded by an assortment of cats. With fur of all colors and sizes, the felines ranged from playful youngsters to old mousers. Some curled up together in cozy piles, others were still roaming and playing.

My mind wandered as I reflected on the strange events that had transpired that day. Evie and I had been caught up in something we could not have expected, and as we talked about what to do next, I saw worry and excitement mingled on her face. Yet despite her unease, there was a sense of wonder and exhilaration amid it all.

A platter that could help humans hear what animals were thinking.

Huh.

Well, we could hear what cats were thinking. Nothing Fiona said and nothing we'd found indicated the platter worked with anything other than cats.

And for all we knew, for sure, maybe just one cat.

I guess I'd have to wait until tomorrow night to discover more.

I sat in the cozy rocking chair and gazed out the window at the birds flitting about our backyard, their calls and songs filling the morning air. The early morning sun was just peeking over the horizon, casting a golden glow over the landscape. With each sip of my hot coffee, I watched as new birds flocked to our feeders, filling me with a sense of wonder and joy at the beauty of the world around me.

It was all so ordinary, so calm and peaceful.

I loved Texas mornings.

Digby—a one-eyed, one-nostriled young tabby tomcat that snored like a chainsaw rigged for overdrive—yawned loudly as he sunned himself on the table next to me. His one good eye slowly closed as he lost himself in the morning's warm sun.

"You know," I said to Digby, "I don't think Evie is wrong about the platter. I kind of want her to be wrong, but I don't think she's wrong." Digby opened his eye lazily, looked at me, and yawned again. I narrowed my eyes at him. "It's just a shame that the world isn't quite ready to know about something like that," I told him. "Think of all the good it could do."

With a slow, sleepy blink, Digby stared at me with uninterested eyes. He lay with his tail curled around himself, his expression showing only indifference and apathy—as if he was unimpressed with whatever I may say or do.

"I know. I know, I know," I said, pretending the cat cared. "I feel like if we could keep the thing away from the people who would want to use it for the wrong reason, it would be fantastic."

Despite my attempts to engage him in conversation, Digby seemed oblivious to my presence; only paying the barest attention as he continued to bask in the heat.

"I would love to know what the pigeons are saying when they argue," I told him. "And the deer, the squirrels, the dogs…"

With a deliberate and slow movement, Digby turned his head toward the window, his eye narrowing as he stared out into the yard. His whiskers twitched and his fur bristled as he scowled, his mouth pulled into a slight frown.

"Well, I'm so sorry I bothered you. You should care, Digby. You know why? Maybe it's possible to give animals a voice. A literal voice. Wouldn't that be great? Don't you think that would be amazing?"

Digby rose slowly from his comfortable seat on the table with his perfect view of the outside, deliberately turning his back on me in a dismissive gesture. He sauntered out of the room with a languid wave of his tail.

"Well, I thought it was interesting, anyway," I chuckled.

Evie entered a moment later, her eyes squinting in the dim light. "Why does it always smell and sound like an alchemist's shop in here?" she grumbled, wrinkling her nose at the powerful aromas of the herbs and oils I had steaming in the background all the time, along with calming white noise. "It's ridiculous to hear owls hooting inside an animal shelter, and every time the crickets chirp, I have an overwhelming desire to tear up the walls to find them."

"Good morning, Sunshine! It keeps the cats calmer," I explained cheerfully, as I had done countless times before. "It's less expensive than using that pheromone diffuser all over the place. We only get so many dona-tions, E." As she pulled down her large pill organizer, I got up and went to get her a cup of coffee.

"Whatever," she mumbled, staring despondently at the pills. The organizer's size dwarfed her iPad because there were so many pills and every morning she seemed unhappy to see them.

"Here you go," I said as cheerfully as I could manage, sliding the mug in front of her. "Do you require anything else, daughter dear?"

She shook her head, her gaze fixed on the pills in front of her.

"Can I get you some breakfast?"

"Not to have to take so many pills," she groused as she shook the container of pills, answering my previous question. "But I don't want to go on a new regimen if it might not work. These work." She turned with a pleading look in her eyes. "Mom, promise me that if I get sick and die, you'll have me cremated and sprinkle my ashes on a mountaintop or something. Or the ocean. A place where I'd want to be, where I'd want to spend eternity. Not in some urn on the mantel that the cats will knock over."

The words seemed to come from a deep well of pain, resonating with a force that left me feeling as if she had punched me in the gut. Things had been going so well lately. My throat tightened, and I struggled to swallow the lump that had formed there. "Oh, dear child, what a way to start a morning," I whispered. I shook my head. "I am not having this conversation. Take your pills."

"But Mom—"

"No," I said, shaking my head as I turned and busied myself with dishes. "I know you're grumpy and off your game first thing in the morning, and my bet is you stayed up too late. If you need to talk about this for real, we can speak about it later." I pointed. "Take your medication."

"I'm not at my best, no, but I just realized I really don't want to be put in an urn and stuck in a box in the storage room with the cat litter." She sighed. "I don't want a funeral. I do not want my friends to stand around and listen to people talk about me as if I'm not dead. So no flowers."

"Okay," I said, instinctively capitulating to her demands. It was easier to agree with her and wait for her pills to stabilize her in the morning than to argue with her or convince her that this discussion was unnecessary. "Whatever you want."

"Good. Thanks." She swallowed a pill—the first of about ten she would take that morning before breakfast. "Now, what I really need is to get a new power converter for my laptop. I love it, but it eats battery bars like they're made of Godiva chocolate."

Early mornings were always the hardest for Evie. Her medication kept her relatively stable and happy most of the time, but it was always a delicate balance. In the early morning, I could usually get her through with a minimum of fuss, but it was always like walking on thin ice; one wrong move and the whole thing could come crashing down.

I stood up and grabbed the coffee pot, spilling hot liquid as I sloppily poured myself a second cup. I took a swig of the scalding brew and grimaced, knowing it was still too hot to drink. I quickly set it back down on the counter, worried that I might burn my mouth if I took too big a gulp.

I hated Evie's bad mornings.

This one, though, wasn't too terrible.

"I need some new clothes, too," she said, checking her pill organizer. "Oh, and I'm out of conditioner. And I need more cat food."

Uh oh.

At that moment, I knew the ideas in her head were simply spinning up at random. Cat food was not something Evie had a lack of access to.

I turned.

Her eyes darted around the room with frenetic energy, quickly taking in the objects within. She didn't focus on anything for long, her gaze flitting from one thing to the next without pausing. Her hands were also constantly moving, picking at her clothes and hair, fidgeting with her glasses, agitated.

"Take a deep breath, sweetie, and slow down, okay? Give your medication a few minutes to kick in."

"Yep. Yep. Yep. I'll do that." She grinned at me as her fingers tapped an erratic beat on the table. "I'll go with you to get the power converter when we go to get the platter." Before I could answer, she swallowed several pills and added, "We're going to go get the platter today, right?"

It was also at that moment I realized Evie's condition might be a problem if we hoped to keep this platter a secret.

Chapter Seven

I WAS STILL SEATED AT THE KITCHEN TABLE, hunched over the newspaper, when I heard the front door open and close. Glancing up, I saw Matt standing in the doorway, a friendly grin on his face. "Miss me?" he asked, sounding amused.

Matt's boyish cheeks were round and rosy, and his crooked smile was infectious. His dark hair was unruly and long, tied back in a ponytail that swayed with each step. As he shrugged off his jacket, his muscular shoulders and arms were revealed, rippling with strength and power.

I adored the kid.

I wished my daughter Evie would adore the kid.

If you get my drift.

"You're here early," I said, glancing at the clock.

Matt hung his jacket on the hook and strode confidently into the living room. "Got up early, thought I'd come in and get the litter boxes for you guys. I know Evie hates to do them, especially in the morning when her meds make her a little dopey." His footsteps echoed in the quiet room as he turned and headed toward the kitchen. "Any coffee or donuts?"

I held up the coffee cup for him to see. "There's a pot made, but no donuts." The disappointment was obvious on his face, and Matt let out a heavy, aggrieved sigh as he turned away from me. "I think there are some English muffins in the fridge."

He opened the refrigerator door and peered inside, then closed it again. "Hmm. I'm hungry, but I have no idea what I want. Well, I kind of know what I want. I want Waffle House. I should get Zippy-eats to deliver Waffle House. Do you want Waffle House? My treat."

These kids and their ability to have anything delivered with a few taps on their phone. In my day, if we wanted Waffle House, we had to go to Waffle House.

Uphill.

Both ways.

In the snow.

"Waffle House is five miles away, Matt. Just go pick it up."

I shifted to make room for him on the couch, and he took a seat beside me. "Naw, easier to get it delivered." Matt's eyes darted around my face as he spoke, and his eyebrows furrowed. "Don't get me wrong, but you look really exhausted, Ms. Rockwell. Like bags under your eyes tired." His gaze seemed intense. "Is Evie okay? Nothing happened to her, did it?"

Why didn't Evie go out with this boy?

He was obviously smitten with her.

"No, nothing like that," I said. I wrapped my hand around the coffee cup and held it carefully as I blew across the hot surface. "Evie's just fine. We got Fiona Blackwell's cat yesterday, and it's always a little stressful when the cat's owner is accused of a crime." As if it happened all the time. "I need to run to the sheriff's office today and talk to Deputy Markham about her."

I didn't specify who the "her" was.

"Right. I totally forgot about that," he said as he scratched the back of his head. "I read about it in the town SocialBook group yesterday and figured they would bring the cat here. How's Belladonna doing?"

I took a sip of my coffee, savoring the rich flavor before thunking the cup onto the table. As I did, I caught Matt's gaze and noticed his expression was a little odd. "You first. You grew up in this town, and you obviously have something rattling around in your head to make your face look like that. What do you know about Fiona and Beau Blackwell?"

He frowned and leaned back. "Well, they had no kids, so I didn't see them around town much when I was growing up. Well, only when Beau went into the store to buy cigarettes. But he wasn't friendly."

"No?" Matt Garcia's grandmother, Estella, owned

Estella's Corner Store, the town's previous one-stop shop in the historic section before Wal-Mart was built.

"Not really. I mean, all my friends thought he was really old and kind of grumpy, so we avoided him. He was already in his sixties when I was a kid."

I nodded. "What does your grandmother Estella think of him? Did she ever say?"

"Oh, she said, all right." He grinned as he remembered. "She told anyone that would listen—and who spoke Spanish—he was a cheating jerk, and that Fiona got a raw deal with that whole thing twenty years ago." His eyes twinkled with amusement. "Grandma Estella called him tramposo whenever he came into the store. 'Es un bastardo tramposo, Mateo.' Beau, being entirely unacquainted with Spanish, thought it was an affectionate nickname or an honorific or something."

I raised an eyebrow. "I can guess what bastardo means. What's tramposo?"

"It means cheater." Matt shrugged, a smile playing on his lips. "She's not exactly what you'd call shy. She's tiny, but she's fierce. She's got a temper too." His eyes twinkled with amusement as he continued. "Anyway, she never understood why this town turned on Fiona Blackwell when Beau Blackwell was the one that lied and cheated."

"So she didn't like him."

"No, she liked Fiona. A lot," he said. "She said Fiona was a saint, and she thought Beau was a loser." He shrugged. "She said just last night it was no big deal that he got killed, either. El karma de Beau estaba atrasado, she said."

"Oh? And that means?"

"His karma was overdue."

"For what he did to Fiona, I suppose."

"She didn't say, but probably." Matt smiled. "Anyway, if Fiona didn't do it, Abuela said it was about time someone did." He pushed stray strands of hair from his face. "I better get to the cat boxes before the kitties riot. Anything I can do for you, Ms. Rockwell?"

"No, Matt, thanks," I said as Evie walked back in.

"Morning, Evie!" Matt's eyes glinted with mischief as he flashed a wide, triumphant grin and winked at Evie. His lips were parted in an unabashed smile as he tilted his head playfully. "You're looking good today, girl!"

Evie blushed red and tried to hide behind her hair.

"You staying with me today or going with your mom?"

"She's going to stay here," I said. I carried my coffee cup to the sink and rinsed it out. "We ran an ad on one of the local news shows this morning, so I'm hoping this afternoon we'll have a few people show up looking to adopt. It'll help if all three of you are here, I think." I turned from the sink and saw Evie frowning at me.

"Three?" Evie asked.

"Darla should be here any minute now," I answered. Before Evie could ask another question, I added, "Evie,

I'm going to go on over to the sheriff's office, okay? You good now?"

She nodded. "I'm good. Sounds like a plan," Evie said, picking up the newspaper and holding it in front of her face. Then she moved her face out from behind it—blocking Matt's view of her expression—and stuck her tongue out at me. "We'll be here when you get back."

I could see the annoyance etched on her features and I wasn't sure if she was annoyed because I asked her if she was good or because I left her there alone with Matt, but I didn't have time to deal with Evie's emotions.

I had to get to the sheriff's office to find out what was going on.

I stepped out of the car and breathed in the clean air of the hill country. The sun was high in the bright blue sky, promising a long day of sun ahead with little possibility of rain. I put on my sunglasses for the short walk to Garcia's Corner Market and grabbed a small grocery store bag from the passenger seat.

It was late morning, and the town was already in full swing as it bustled with people going about their busy lives.

The old town center of my small Central Texas town was a quaint and charming little area lined with old-fashioned storefronts and buzzing with activity. The buildings were painted in bright colors, many displaying ornate wooden signs out front advertising the businesses that occupied the ground floor.

One building was Estrella Garcia's small grocery store, a community staple that carried a broad selection of food, including freshly prepared products like hamburgers, grilled ribeye sandwiches, and fresh home-made salsa. There was also a great selection of wines and regional beer from local brewers.

I had hoped to run into Matt's grandmother, Estella, but she wasn't in that morning. It wasn't surprising. The woman had to be in her midseventies by now, and how she ran a grocery store at her age was beyond me.

I browsed through the store for a few minutes, picking out some donuts for Matt and Deputy Markham, before heading up to the counter to pay for my groceries.

"Cecelia, are you all right?" asked the cashier, Sadie Taggart, looking concerned.

"How can anyone be okay after something like this?" Cecelia Goddard, a local real estate agent, replied, shaking her head in disbelief. She held herself with an air of authority, as if she was used to her statements being taken as gospel with no questions. "The mayor must be absolutely devastated. I just don't understand how something like this could happen here in our little town." Her voice lowered, she whispered, "I always knew Fiona Blackwell was crazy."

Sadie, an elderly woman with kind, creased features and thin, graying hair that frames her face, nodded sympathetically. "I know, it's terrible," she said. "But the mayor is a strong woman and I'm sure she'll get through this."

Cecelia sighed heavily and ran her hand through her dark brown hair. "I hope so," she said. "Poor Jessa. This kind of tragedy can really take its toll on a person. After all he put her through, too." She paused for a moment before continuing, "But at least the police seem to have things under control now. Tablerock PD's got someone out there investigating the murder, so I guess they're making progress."

"Out where?" I asked before I could stop myself.

Cecelia turned and looked at me, her sharp business suit barely creasing with the movement. I wondered how much starch this woman used. "Out at Wardwell Manor. How that woman could live alone in that gigantic home all these years is just beyond me. Beyond me! I'm sure they'll find whatever they're looking for," she said, and then added with a hint of heartlessness, "and they will fry that nasty Fiona Blackwell for all she's done."

Tablerock Police had handed the case over to the county, though. Rather than point that out, I said, "You seem awfully sure Fiona Blackwell is guilty."

Cecelia shook her head in disbelief. "Like you don't? Please, Eleanor, be serious," she asked. "The police have been investigating Beau Blackwell's murder for days now, and they must know what they're doing. They don't just put someone in jail for no reason at all."

I struggled not to raise my eyebrows at that one.

"I have to get going." She leaned down and grabbed her bag of groceries. "I just hope they get this whole thing wrapped up as quickly as possible. The commission on Wardwell Manor is going to be incredible."

"Commission?" I frowned. "What commission?"

Cecelia acted coy as she brushed off my question about the commission, refusing to elaborate any further. Instead, she hurried out of the store with her bag of groceries and a sly smile on her face, leaving me standing alone at the counter.

I turned to the cashier, feeling frustrated. "What commission was she talking about? Do you know?" I asked.

"Cecelia Goddard is friends with Mayor Jessa Winthrop," Sadie said, feigning discomfort as her eager eyes sparkled at the chance to pass on gossip. "Now, you didn't hear it from me, but she seemed to imply earlier—and I don't know how or why—that they both stand to make a lot of money from Wardwell Manor now that Fiona's been arrested. But I just don't see how."

I didn't see how, either.

Texas was a community property state. Fiona and Beau owned their home, as far as I knew, and with Beau gone, Fiona solely owned it. She did not forfeit her home just because she was suspected of murdering her husband.

And why would Mayor Jessa Winthrop have anything to do with Fiona's house?

As I approached the front desk at the sheriff's office, Deputy Markham stood and watched me. His face was friendly, but as I got closer, his expression faded to a solemn one. "Hey, Ms. Rockwell," he said, putting his pen down. "Is everything okay with Belladonna?"

The deputy's voice was warm and musical, with a slight southern drawl. From his firm jaw and chiseled cheekbones to his kind, intelligent eyes, his features were smooth and well-defined. His broad shoulders exuded a rugged sense of confidence and charm against the dark wood-paneled office backdrop.

Oh, if only I were younger.

And thinner.

And...

Well, anyway.

I smiled as I answered, "Belladonna's just fine. She's eating well and seems content with our place. I'm not sure why she wasn't all that happy with you, Deputy, but she's been as sweet as pie since we got her."

The deputy's face relaxed, and he chuckled, "Well, I'm glad to hear she's doing well." He nodded, then grew silent for a moment. "I told you, I'm not really a cat person. Maybe she knew that somehow."

I glanced back toward Sheriff Dixon's satellite office.

Even when we had the only murder in the county, it was empty.

As usual.

The police station was a charming structure with a classic red brick exterior and a wide front veranda. A string of rocking chairs and a smooth southern porch swing dotted the veranda, inviting visitors to rest and enjoy the peaceful atmosphere. The front door was made of sturdy wood and featured a large glass window at the top, which was framed by decorative molding. Despite its small size, the structure blended in with the rustic countryside, exuding an odd sense of calm and ease for a police station.

I shrugged and leaned against the front desk. "Well, she's a cat. They're very instinctive animals, so it is possible. She won't waste time fretting over it. I promise you that."

"Glad to hear it. Well, if the cat's fine, what brings you in today?" he asked after a beat.

I was opening my mouth to answer when I heard a loud commotion coming from outside.

In a sudden flurry of movement, Deputy Markham jumped out from behind the counter and drew his gun. His eyes were alert and his body was tense, as if he was bracing for a confrontation. The commotion outside grew louder, and it sounded like someone was shouting.

The air was charged with tension and anticipation.

"What's going on out there, Markham?" one detective asked.

Without answering, the deputy moved swiftly toward the door.

I followed.

A group of people gathered across the street, near the park. Maybe five people, could be ten. They were red-faced and pointing, and it looked like the group was arguing with someone. It was hard to see—and more people arrived from all directions to confront...

A tall young man, dressed all in black, with a shaved head and a mohawk haircut. He backed away slowly, arms raised in the air. His eyes were wide with fear, and he looked desperate and terrified. I didn't recognize him.

One of the mob cocked their arm back and hurled a rock.

"Stop!" I shouted. I winced, horrified, as it hit the mohawked kid in the chest with a sickening thud. "What are you doing?"

He staggered backward in shock.

The movement brought him up against Dr. Canter, the local pediatrician, and the doc reached out with concern to steady him. With breathless words, the spikey-headed young man mumbled an apology and pushed him away, turning to run into the wooded park.

Half of the crowd followed him, still shouting and gesturing.

"What on earth is going on?" I asked no one in particular.

"Son of a—" The deputy glanced down at me. "—nutcracker," Markham muttered, starting down the steps. His lips pressed together, his eyes narrowed, and his hands clenched into fists. He said, "Stay here, Ms. Rockwell."

"Go, Deputy! I'm fine."

Markham's face was a blank mask of concentration as he darted across the street and vanished into what now looked like a sea of people.

The spring sunlight bathed me in a weirdly comforting golden glow while the warm Texas breeze whispered against my face. It was oddly peaceful as I waited on the station porch, my foot tapping impatiently on the weathered wood.

That's when I heard the gunshot.

It was sharp and sudden, like the crack of a small branch breaking underfoot, or a firecracker going off in a silent room. The echo of the shot bounced through me. My heart leaped into my throat and I froze for a moment before sprinting in the direction it had come from.

Yes, I know.

I know what you're thinking.

Now, I am fifty and fat and run a cat rescue from my home. My back's been bad for years, it makes me limp and shuffle my walk sometimes. You think I shouldn't go near that sound, don't you?

I mean, I knew I shouldn't go near that sound.

I knew it.

There were two choices that day: run toward it or away from it.

In the end, my curiosity was stronger than my fear.

So I did, in fact, run across the street.

Well.

Run may be a slight exaggeration.

I raced down the street, desperate to discover what was happening, to see for myself the source of all the commotion. My breath came in ragged gasps and my feet dragged through the hot, sticky street, struggling to keep up with my frantic movements.

Every instinct screamed for me to flee, but I had to know what was going on. So I kept moving, pulled toward the crowd by a compulsion I didn't understand.

I felt it in my bones.

As I pushed my way through the boisterous crowd, I noticed the crowd was gathered around something...still. There was something odd about it. Unnatural, even—I began to sense a chill in the warm air as I strode closer. Amid the grim expressions, I looked down and saw a still, unmoving body at the center of the crowd.

Fiona Blackwell.

"No," I whispered.

Detective Markham got down on one knee and pressed his index finger into her neck. He performed a slow, methodical search, but by the look on his face I knew what the outcome would be.

She was dead.

Tears welled up in my eyes, and I shook.

This could not happen.

And yet I could see that it did.

I'd barely spoken to the woman, barely understood who she was or what the silver platter thing was. I felt like a bucket of iced water had been thrown at me.

Deputy Markham quietly shut Fiona's eyes.

Chapter Eight

I F EVERYTHING HAD SEEMED FAR-FETCHED UP TO
this point—and considering we had magical drink trays
and talking cats, it had seemed very far-fetched—things
had really gone off the rails by the time Fiona Blackwell
was shot.

Right in front of the police station.

In a park that sits in full view of every cop our small
town has.

I mean, what the hell? Who does that?

And what was she even doing there?

I ran my hands through my hair, trying to calm
myself down. I couldn't afford to let my emotions get the
best of me. I had to stay calm, to figure out a plan for
dealing with this situation.

I couldn't let my panic get the better of me.

As the coroner approached, his eyes were cold and

unsympathetic as he silently lifted Fiona's limp body onto the gurney. Other police officers stood nearby, their gazes intense and accusatory as they questioned the crowd gathered to watch the scene.

Deputy Markham, I noticed, looked frustrated, scowling as he sought answers from those around him. Most claimed they only saw the commotion and not what happened or who was shot.

"I watched that vandal we were trying to grab!" JD Lance told Markham. "I didn't even know Fiona was here with us. Isn't she supposed to be in jail?"

Vandal?

Why would a mob chase a vandal in front of a police station?

"Not one of you thought to go into that building right over there"— Deputy Markham pointed at the station, clearly irritated—"and get a police officer? You all just went vigilante?" His face was flushed. "None of you saw anything while you were playing Batman?" Silence. "Anyone know who the guy was you were chasing?"

The assembled townsfolk looked sheepish and averted their gazes, clearly aware they had acted reck-lessly. No one fessed up to throwing the rock at the man running away from the scene. No one saw anyone with a gun. No one saw who shot Fiona.

In disbelief, Deputy Markham shook his head.

I felt a twinge of pity for him. Seldom had I encountered a homicide scene so brimming with onlookers, and yet so sparse on details. Even in the glaring sun, something shady was clearly afoot.

Not that I'd encountered a homicide scene before. But I watched television, and this never happened on Law & Order.

Dr. Canter made his way toward me, his dark eyes darting across the street, clutching a small leather case. He leaned in close; his breath was sour with coffee and cigarette smoke. "When you think about it, it seems a little strange," he whispered.

Ugh. I caught a strong whiff of the good doctor's Drakkar Noir cologne and wondered how many kids in this town get allergies the moment they walk into the pediatrician's office. Leaning back, I responded, "Oh? What does?"

He moved in even closer, so close I could see the beads of sweat on his brow. "There were at least twenty people here, and no one knows who that guy is?"

"Probably one of them folk from Austin," someone piped up.

"True, that is strange," I agreed.

Sure, it was strange.

And obvious.

"But there's something even stranger," I said, my voice reverberating through the crowd. I leaned away from him, trying to get away from the cloud of his cologne. "Fiona Blackwell was in jail as of yesterday. I saw her during visiting hours, and she seemed to plan on staying for a while. How did she get here to be killed?"

Deputy Markham looked at me sharply.

But no one—not the deputy, and not the crowd—responded.

When Fiona's body was removed, most people left (after explaining to Markham which of their neighbors did what, how, and when.)

I remained close enough to hear the conversations and overheard when Markham requested more detailed statements from the two or three individuals closest to Fiona. When asked to describe the runner they were chasing, they all described very young men.

If eyewitness statements were this untrustworthy, I wonder how the police ever caught anyone for anything.

"What exactly are you doing in this part of town, Eleanor?" Dr. Canter said this with a wildly inappropriate smirk, almost making me roll my eyes. Because of his career and money, the fifty-nine-year-old single doctor seemed to believe that his uninvited familiarity would be welcomed by every middle-aged woman in town. "Isn't your house closer to Woodville?" He went on, leaning in too close again.

"I was paying Detective Markham a visit. I had a few questions about Fiona—Silver Circle is looking after Fiona's cat, Belladonna, while she's in—well, was in jail."

I cast a glance at the deputy. "I'll have to find out which lawyer is handling her will."

Questions I never asked, and which were pointless now.

Because she was dead.

How the hell did that happen?

"Are you all right, Eleanor?"

Sure.

I had a pesky talking cat and a departed woman who had taken the answers I needed with her to the grave, but sure. I was just dandy.

I took a deep, shaky breath in an attempt to steady my racing heart. My mind reeled with questions and I could feel the sweltering pressure of the Texas sun on my skin as droplets of sweat started to form on my forehead.

Why was she out of jail?

Who released her?

"Eleanor?" Dr. Canter prompted with a furrowed brow.

"Sorry. I was just thinking." I turned away as I spoke. When I looked back up at the doctor, he was staring at me with a curious expression. "What? I'm fine, Tony. Don't trouble yourself."

Dr. Canter's hard eyes narrowed as they roved my face, as if he was trying to determine whether I was telling the truth. I kept my face expressionless, waiting for him to lose interest. Finally, his lips thinned into a tight line as he muttered something too low for me to catch while turning away.

The road ahead stretched out like a ribbon of asphalt, cutting through the landscape as I raced along in my car. I tried to keep my focus on the road, thoughts whirling through my mind as I struggled to make sense of the events of the day.

Hell, the week.

They had murdered Fiona in cold blood, whoever they were, and the image of her dead stare would not leave my mind. I'd left the shelter determined to find answers to questions, but now?

There were simply more questions.

Why was Fiona out of jail?

Her escape should have been impossible, and it didn't seem like the police had released her. Putting all that aside, why someone would want to shoot her in broad daylight was even less clear.

Revenge for Beau?

Covering up what happened to Beau?

Maybe she really didn't do it.

Maybe the person that killed Beau didn't want her cleared.

And I still couldn't get away from this—who the heck shoots someone right across from a police station? There have to be security cameras around there, right?

"Stop it," I said out loud. "You need to take this one step at a time."

I spent the rest of the drive trying to calm my racing thoughts.

When I pulled into my driveway, I noticed Landon's gold Chevy truck parked in the lot. He was sitting on the front steps, his thick arms propped on his knees, his head in his hands—hands so large they looked like they could twist steel or crush bone if he was angry enough.

"Hello, Landon," I said as I approached the house. "Did we have a delivery today?"

Landon, the resident carpenter of Tablerock, was an expert at creating high-end interior features. He might have been well known for his crown molding, customized doors, and fancy coffers, but to us he was the mastermind behind our custom (and donated) cat furniture. His expertise in wainscoting and wall paneling were rivaled only by his flair for making feline-friendly retreats, cat trees, and custom catios (patios for cats.).

Landon Rogers, tough guy, had a thing for cats.

He looked up, his face bruised and bloody.

I gasped. "Landon! What happened?"

"I almost got that jackrabbit thug with Miss Fiona. Chased him all the way into the thicket, right over the creek, but just when I had him, he turned around and busted my face in," Landon said gruffly by way of greeting. "I saw you at the shooting, thought I'd come over here and make sure you were okay, but"—he pointed at his bruised face—"I didn't want to go in and scare Ellie with my face."

So instead, Landon sat on my porch to scare anyone who wanted to adopt a cat.

Got it.

"You were downtown when Fiona Blackwell got shot?" I asked and then added, "Are you hurt anywhere else?" I was concerned that the man might need medical attention.

"Nah. Just my face." He rubbed gingerly at the swollen area just under his eye, and his good eye narrowed in a mix of pain and anger. "He got me one good time with this rock, but it looks like I'll live." Landon smiled, but I could see the pain behind it. "I'm just not sure about my face. I don't think that's gonna buff out."

"Well, I've got some experience with cleaning up wounds. On cats. But the principle's the same," I said. "Come on up. I'll get you cleaned up, and we'll get some ice on your face."

I extended my hand.

"Why, thank you, lady," Landon said, clutching my hand gently but pulling himself up to his feet without using me at all. "It's much appreciated."

Once inside, I grabbed soap and paper towels and lathered them under the kitchen faucet. "Sit down at the table and take your hat off," I told Landon.

He did.

I stood over him. "Tilt your head up."

He did.

"What did you see happen downtown?" I asked as I cleaned the blood off his jaw, my brow furrowed in concern.

Landon winced as I did it.

"That hurt?" I asked, my eyes wide with worry.

"Nah, just stung is all."

"You sure?"

He nodded. "I don't know what happened, Ellie. I was trying to get the guy in the leg—you know I trained with Waldo Monroe at the park, and he taught me to go for the arms and legs—but I was too late, and he just turned and got me with a full-strength punch while holding a rock. He was strong." Landon's eyes hardened as he recounted the event, and his fists clenched.

Waldo Monroe was the local martial arts teacher. He taught karate in the park a few times a week. Or maybe it was judo. Or something that ended in itsu. I wasn't sure.

"You didn't recognize him?" I asked.

"By name? Nope." Landon's eyes narrowed, and he angrily shoved his black hair out of his face. "Though I don't know if I would. I used to know everybody in this town, but now? Too many city folks are moving here."

I tried not to look offended since, by Landon's definition, I was a city folk that moved here.

"I didn't really see him all that well, though," he continued. "I'd say he was about my size—long hair, a black t-shirt with some weird circle design on it, tattoos, a huge guy. I have seen him before, though."

"Oh?"

"Yeah. Once at the supermarket, and then I saw him at the sporting goods store. He was looking at a bow and arrow with Doc Canter. You know those fancy compound bows that people use for hunting? Yeah, one of those."

My eyebrows scrunched together in confusion. "With Tony Canter? The pediatrician? You're sure?"

Landon nodded, his face serious.

Dr. Canter said nothing about recognizing the runner. And I was sure when Don Markham questioned him, he swore he'd never seen him before. In fact, the doctor could barely recall anything about the guy. "When was that?"

"Just last weekend, actually. I was in the next department over in the camping section, replacing my—"

"I just want to be clear. You saw the man you chased away from a murder scene in Bowell's Sporting Goods with the town pediatrician? You're absolutely sure?" I interrupted, disbelief clear in my voice.

"Yes," he said, his expression solemn. "Just because you asked me twice, it ain't gonna change my answer, Ellie."

"Sorry. There, that's better. At least now it shouldn't get infected." I stepped back. "Why were you all chasing that guy, anyway?"

"He broke a window on JD Lance's brand new pickup truck with a rock."

Plausible.

Men in this town took their brand new pickup trucks seriously.

I moved toward the sink to wash my hands. I suddenly realized as I lathered that Landon took martial arts with a few cops from Tablerock. "Hey, question—do you know how Beau died, Landon?" I asked, without turning around.

"No, ma'am. News reports said police hadn't released the cause of death. Last I heard, anyway. Maybe they're still investigating."

I glanced over at him, and his confusion was obvious, like he'd never expected me to ask for gossip and conspiracy theories instead of confirmed and documented facts from the local paper. He scratched his head, an age-old gesture that had probably been around since the days of cavemen.

Men.

I grabbed the Tablerock paper. "They know enough to arrest someone for a murder, though." I scanned the article I'd opened. "Lots of speculation, but no comment from the police on the cause of death. Hey! You know some of these cops, right?" I waved the paper. "Have they said anything about why they won't say anything?"

I turned around, and Landon was standing much closer than I expected.

He was much closer than anyone should be to any other person not their spouse or mother.

Without thinking, I took a full step back and my elbow struck the counter strip in front of the cast iron sink, sending pain up my arm. Unfortunately for me, it landed squarely on my funny bone. "Ow!" I cried out, my hand going to my elbow.

Landon stepped back quickly, looking mortified. "I'm sorry, Ellie. Didn't mean to crowd you," he said gruffly. Landon's good eye was wide with concern, and his body angled toward me. "You okay? Want me to get you some of that ice?"

"It's fine, really. I'm fine."

I knew Landon was interested in me.

He'd made it clear every time he looked at me with those piercingly intense eyes of his. Well, that and the way he asked me out on a date six months ago.

When I turned him down, I could see the disappointment in his eyes, but he didn't press the issue. He simply shrugged his shoulders and walked away.

If I dated a man at fifty years old, Landon Rogers would be exactly the type of man I would date. He was ruggedly handsome, with a strong jawline and broad shoulders. He knew how to build a shelf—and that, my friends, is no small quality in a man. He was divorced—but only once—and despite his divorce, he kept in contact with his kids. He liked animals. He liked cats.

But I would not date a man.

Ever. Why?

Because Evie would never move out. Never.

I mean, I wouldn't stand in her way if she wanted to, and I'd do everything I could to help her, but my daughter stated repeatedly (and unequivocally) that she would never leave. When her illness worsened, she appreciated the security and safety net that my presence provided. She wasn't sure how she would handle it on her own.

To be honest, I wasn't sure if Evie stayed with me because she couldn't make it on her own, had resigned herself to never making it on her own, or was too afraid to fail.

But in some ways, it didn't matter.

It would not happen. I couldn't imagine asking a man I dated to deal with it. Especially not at my age. Hell, Evie's father couldn't even deal with it.

I liked Landon and everything, but he was my friend.

That's all he—or any man—would ever be.

Landon—who'd been watching me, silent as a grave, while my brain worked overtime—tilted his head to the side and flashed me a smirk. "What?"

"Nothing," I replied quickly, trying to hide my resigned expression. "I'm going to make some coffee. You want some?"

"Sure, thanks. You gonna read the paper?" he asked, gesturing toward the Tablerock Independent still clutched in my hand.

"No. I'm not really reading it. I just wanted to check

the cause of death of Beau Blackwell," I told him as I turned on the coffee pot and then waved at the newspaper. "I thought maybe they'd released more details I'd missed. But nope."

"Yeah. The cops are being weird with it. At least, it seems that way to me. Figuring out what happened is like trying to solve a jigsaw puzzle where you can't see the picture on the box," he said.

"Why do you say that?" I asked, my brow furrowed in concern.

"I had coffee at Dale's this morning." Dale's Donutteria was a popular breakfast spot known for its finely crafted coffee. Filled with the aromas of fresh pastries and brewing beans, the shop was always a busy hub of activity in the mornings, with people lining up to grab a quick bite before heading off to work. "I saw Mario Lopez sitting with some of the other cops, so I went over. You know, just to be friendly."

"Okay."

"Well, they were friendly back. Until I asked how the case was going."

"Oh?"

"They all snapped their mouths shut like a door slamming in spring storm winds. It felt like they were hiding something, but not in the normal way. If that makes any sense," Landon said as he sat down and rested his elbows on the table. He had an uncharacteristically worried look on his face. "It was odd."

I nodded in agreement as I looked down at the front page.

"Maybe I should tell Markham what I saw at the sporting goods store?"

"Maybe. Or I can tell him if you like. You should probably get home, take some Tylenol, and lay down." I still needed to get the details from the deputy and figure out who was handling Fiona's probate case. Even though cats have their own perspectives, they are still considered property under the law. It was likely going to be my responsibility to find Belladonna a suitable home. "I can mention it then."

Landon nodded and stood up. As he went to put his hat back on, it tumbled from his hand. I caught it before it hit the floor and he grabbed it from my hands with an embarrassed smile. "Thank you," he said, placing it firmly back on his head. "You call me if you need me, you hear, Ellie?"

I assured him I would.

His expression told me he knew I wouldn't.

Once Landon was gone, I sat at the table and worried.

What on earth was going on with all this?

Two murders in one month was more than enough for a small town like Tablerock, and now there was a mob running after some goth kid in front of the police station? I wanted to stay as far away from the crimes and investigations as possible, and I wondered if it was possible considering Fiona's cat was just two rooms away.

I sighed and looked toward the isolation room.

I could see Belladonna, Fiona's sleek black cat, through the window. She was lying on the cat tree and breathing contentedly as she slept. I could feel my heart constrict as I realized I needed to tell her that her owner had gone forever.

With another sigh, I got up and made my way to Belladonna's room.

Chapter Nine

It felt like the days just zoomed by in the rescue center, with endless scoops of litter, stacks of dishes, and, of course, the near-endless stream of cats that came through.

But no matter how hard I worked to distract myself, no matter how much time had passed since that day when Fiona got shot, I couldn't shake the feeling that something was still off.

A week had gone by since that fateful afternoon, and while I didn't ignore it, I just assumed Deputy Markham would return my phone call (or Fiona's probate attorney would come to find me) to discuss Belladonna.

But a whole week went by, and no one did.

"Is she any better?" I asked Evie the following bright Wednesday morning as I absently scratched a lost tabby behind his ears. The tabby's eyes were closed as it blissfully enjoyed the feel of my hand scratching its head.

"Belladonna's still sullen, relatively unresponsive," she blurted, not looking up at me, her voice muted as she made herself a cup of coffee. "If I wasn't on antidepressants, I think I might go find the nearest bridge to jump off just looking at her. It's just...I mean, it's heartbreaking." Her eyes were dark, and her movements jerky as she spooned sugar into her cup. "I swear, Mom, mornings are hard enough for me. Facing her just makes me want to cry. I've never seen an animal change so much. From totally regal to just—"

"I know. She's an old cat, honey, and she'd been with Fiona for almost twenty years." My statement didn't comfort my daughter. I could see the pain in Evie's eyes.

"I know."

The cat was skittish with me after I had informed Belladonna of Fiona Blackwell's untimely passing. Evie, being the kind soul she was, attempted to assuage the feline's sorrow and settled into the task of raising the poor creature's spirits. "It's very hard for animals that have been with someone their whole lives to lose them."

"I know." She sighed and took a sip of her coffee. "But she's going to have to get used to it," Evie snapped, turning to face me. "I mean, I'm not stupid."

It would happen like that.

A subtle energy change, a response with a tone that seemed a little more out of place then it should be. A little more frustrated. I softened my expression, hoping I could gently tether my daughter to the reality she was becoming overwhelmed by. To everyone else, it looked like a petulant adult that just didn't know how to handle things.

But I knew.

"I didn't say you were, sweetheart," I replied quietly, and then raised my hands in a gesture of surrender.

"No, I know you didn't. It's just..." Evie breathed deeply, desperate to get a hold of herself. "Mom, it's hard. It's hard seeing her like that, and I don't know what to do. I put her on that table thing, and either it's broken or she won't talk to me." Evie's voice broke, and she put her hand over her mouth. She was becoming more and more agitated. "I don't know what to do. I want to help her, and nothing I do seems to snap her out of it."

It was ironic, this statement coming from my daughter.

The heart condition Evie was born with had brought her three open heart surgeries before she'd hit her teen years, each one longer and more complicated than the last. By the third one, she'd learned to handle it. She knew no different.

The brain damage from the last surgery, though?

That was the real challenge.

We had no idea it had been there for several years. It was a silent, sneaky souvenir we brought home that tripped my daughter up at the most unexpected times. I'd assumed Evie had turned into a spoiled brat who didn't care enough about me to remember to take out the trash, clean her room, or do her homework.

In reality, she'd had a series of small strokes during her heart surgery that had gone undetected until an MRI revealed the tiny blood flow outages that had caused little patches of damage. Those little patches created barriers in her brain she would run into unexpectedly several times a day, like a cartoon character slamming into a tunnel painted on a brick wall.

Sometimes, Evie could work her way around it, over the top, under it.

Sometimes, she couldn't.

"We'll take Belladonna to the vet," I said, putting a step in front of her I hoped she could fixate on. "Maybe Laurie can give us something to help her."

My daughter's eyes darted around the room. "Yes. Laurie. I hope so."

"Ms. Rockwell?" Darla's voice called from the front of the house.

"In the kitchen, Darla!"

"There's someone here!" she called back.

I quickly checked the time. It was just after 7 a.m., and I couldn't believe someone was in such a rush to adopt. Actually, someone here this early was likely abandoning their cat. "Can you take care of the intake?" I called back, my worried eyes focused on Evie as she fought to keep her composure.

"It's not an intake. Mayor Jessa Winthrop is here to see you."

The Tablerock mayor. Here?

"Fantastic," I muttered under my breath and then

looked over at Evie. "Are you going to be okay? I can stay here with you for a bit if you need me to."

"I'm fine!" she snapped angrily, her face reddening with embarrassment. "I'm not a child." She gestured toward the door. "I'm coming with you."

With a sigh and a forced smile, I went into the front room to see what the mayor wanted so early in the morning.

Jessa Winthrop strutted into the shelter's foyer, making it crystal clear she was a woman to be reckoned with. A rhinestone-studded cowboy hat sat atop her platinum blond curls, and a buttery yellow dress hugged curves that were more pronounced than nature had intended. Her look was like something out of a country-and-western club fundraiser for the affluent silver-haired set or schmoozing rich donors on a yacht on Lake Travis.

It was a sight to behold, although perhaps one that should have been kept under wraps of a looser cut and a more neutral color than butter yellow.

"Mayor Winthrop," I said, extending my hand. "How nice to see you."

She pulled her hand from her purse and instead planted it on her hip with an exasperated sigh. "I'm going to have to cut out the 'Mayor Winthrop' part of this equation, honey. My nephew, Jackson, tells me you have my cat Belladonna and her fancy antique tabletop."

Evie and I exchanged a look, both of us struggling to keep straight faces. "I'll need them both back." She gazed at me, her eyes narrowed as she took in every detail of my expression. "Well, what are you waiting for? Now, please. I don't have all day."

I dropped my hand as Evie and I glanced at one another.

The nerve of this woman.

"It's always a pleasure to see you, Mayor," I said as pleasantly as I could fake. "As you may or may not be aware, Deputy Markham brought the cat to us when he arrested Fiona Blackwell. To release her to anyone, I'd need a court order, or a written order from Deputy Markham or the county."

"Nonsense!" Her mouth was set in a firm line, her brow furrowed with tension and anxiety. "I'm the mayor, and I'm telling you—that's my cat."

I disliked politicians, and this woman was showing all the reasons I disliked politicians.

"Really? That's not what the cat says," Evie said behind me.

Oh, dear.

"What did you say, young lady?" Mayor Jessa snapped, leaning forward and glaring at Evie. "You want to repeat that?"

"I said that the cat's microchip says otherwise, ma'am," my daughter told the mayor. "Fiona Blackwell is clearly registered as the cat's legal owner."

"Mayor Winthrop," I said as respectfully as I could

manage while wanting to punch the arrogant woman in the nose, "we'll have to have a longer discussion later if you want to adopt the cat." I paused. "If the cat should come up for adoption, that is."

A much longer discussion.

Involving multiple home visits.

So many home visits that by the time I'm done, the cat will probably have passed away before having to spend a single moment with you.

"Adoption?" she asked, shocked.

"Yes, ma'am. For the moment, she is staying in the shelter." Evie nodded in agreement. "As I'm sure you're aware, we have to follow the law."

She glared at me.

I tried to look calm as I forced a smile onto my face. "Thank you so much for stopping by to check on Belladonna, Mayor Winthrop. Is there anything else we can help you with?"

She leaned forward and fixed me with an irritatingly smug expression, her hands resting imperiously on her hips. The smirk was plastered on her face almost as strongly as that garish layer of blush she always wore. "I know the law. I'm the mayor. Of course, I know the law. That's why I'm telling you to give me Belladonna."

My patience ran out at that point.

"No, ma'am."

"The sheriff's order says Bella stays here," Evie added.

Darla watched the exchange silently.

"Is that what the order says? Well, maybe it does, and maybe it doesn't," she mused. The mayor's face was red with anger, her hands clenched into fists. She stepped forward into my personal space, but I didn't back away. "Eleanor, Fiona's dead. No one cares. Just give me the damn cat."

Eleanor?

Were we buddies suddenly?

"Mayor Winthrop, again—if you'd like to adopt the cat, I suggest you be patient. There's nothing I can do until the sheriff's department or the courts direct me on what the next steps are. Until then, by law, Belladonna stays with us." I tilted my head. "I assure you, we take wonderful care of all the cats. She'll be fine."

Mayor Winthrop glared at me, stepping up ominously until we were nose to nose.

I locked eyes with her, and a shudder ran through me as I felt an unspoken battle of wills brewing between us as we faced off.

The tension finally broke when Mayor Winthrop snorted dismissively and turned on her glittery four-inch heels, stalking out the front door.

"What the heck was that?" Darla asked.

"What on earth was that all about?" Evie chimed in.

"If you're both asking me, I have no idea," I said, glancing out the window.

"I have to tell you, Ms. Rockwell, it's rare people go toe to toe telling off a politician and have the politician retreat," Darla said. "I can't believe she acted that way. She acted like she owned the place."

We watched as Mayor Winthrop barged through my garden, her designer shoes crushing Evie's petunias.

"Well, that was rude," I mumbled.

Her piercing eyes blazed with fury as she bellowed at whomever was on the other side of her cell phone, punctuating each of her angry words with wild jabs of her finger for emphasis.

"Who could she be talking to?" Darla wondered.

I couldn't make out the conversation, but it was clear the mayor was none too pleased.

"Damn," Evie said. "She's pissed."

With one last ferocious look in our direction, she got in her car and slammed the door shut.

"I don't think that woman hears the word 'no' very often. And Darla, people go toe to toe with politicians all the time," I said. "I need to call Deputy Markham and let him know that Mayor Winthrop claims that Belladonna is hers. Maybe he knows what this is about."

"Didn't you do that already, and didn't he not bother to call you back?" Evie asked, raising an eyebrow.

"I did, but he was probably just busy, Evie."

"What are you going to tell him?" my daughter asked.

"That she needs a restraining order on the mayor," Darla joked.

I smirked. "Just that Mayor Winthrop came here this

morning and claimed she was the rightful owner of Belladonna and that I'm still not sure what comes next."

I watched Belladonna sleep, her small frame curled tightly into itself like a frightened shrimp. She seemed so vulnerable, yet her paws were twitching like she was fending off an invisible attacker. I couldn't help but wonder what secrets lay dormant in her mind.

I've met plenty of pets whose owners have died. It's never easy to help them through it. They don't understand—can't understand—why the person they love (who is their entire world) has suddenly vanished.

They accept eventually. And they mourn.

But they never really comprehend.

She stirred, and her eyes opened. A soft meow fell from her lips.

Evie was right.

Belladonna was in a dangerously low depression.

I rose from my seat and steadily made my way to the cat tree where she rested. I ran my hand over her fur and she recoiled, clearly distressed by my touch. I left my hand there a few inches from her, waiting.

"I don't know if you can understand me when I talk," I whispered. "I don't know how that platter works, and I don't know if you can understand English when you're not standing on it, but I want you to know you will be okay."

She twisted her head, rubbing her cheek briefly against my hand.

"You're a wonderful cat," I whispered. "A great cat. I know it feels like the world's come crashing down around you. You've been handed a raw deal because humans can be jerks." I smiled sadly. "It'll get better, though. I promise I'll help you through it. If you let me."

I didn't know if she understood me. I hoped she could. It would be nice to think that she could understand me and that she might try to trust me. Cats that didn't eat and didn't drink didn't live long, and her food and water bowls were suspiciously full.

She stood up and walked toward the edge of the cat tree—her home for the last week—as if I'd jolted her to action with my thoughts.

"What are you doing?" I asked quietly.

Belladonna jumped down and walked slowly across the isolation room toward the platter, which was in the farthest corner of the small room opposite the door. I placed it there so she could use it if she wanted, but so the small table would conceal it from anyone who opened the door and peered inside.

She crept up to it cautiously, each measured step calculating. Then, with a haughty arch of her tail, Belladonna made three full rotations around the platter before sashaying back to the cat tree with purpose. She scaled the levels with a grace that belied her size and nestled herself deep into the first level's plush square cubby.

"Okay," I said to myself, looking back and forth between the silver circle plate and the cat tree. "You want me to put the platter on the first level?"

With a languid yawn, she fixed me with a look I could adequately describe as Well, duh. Then she left the first level and hopped up to the second one.

The brilliant, gleaming silver of the metallic circle reflected the light coming from the window. I picked it up, immediately noticing the strange coolness of the crystalline inlay as I wrapped my fingers around it. After removing it from its hiding spot between the wooden table and wall, I delicately placed it within its new sanctuary—perched on the first level of Belladonna's cozy cubby.

"Okay," I said, watching Belladonna. "I moved it. See?" I tapped one level below her. "Now what?"

The cat rolled her eyes slowly over me like a queen inspecting a peasant. Her head dropped to one side, her damp nose twitching as she looked me over. She showed no intention of moving from the highest perch of the cat tree.

I waited patiently, watching her.

I mean, she's still a cat. Magic talking disk or not.

With cats, you have to be patient.

So I was.

Seconds ticked by.

Then minutes.

Finally, I got up, walked to the door, and reached for

the handle. "Okay, you didn't maul me with those foot needles, at least," I told her. "That's progress."

As the handle clicked, a soft female voice stopped me.

"Wait."

Belladonna lay sprawled across the platter, her tail lazily wrapped around her. The cubbyhole was drenched in a radiant yellow (similar, I noted, to Mayor Winthrop's too-tight dress.) I could tell that Belladonna's suggestion had been a clever one. It looked less like a magical platter and more like a decoration or a warming light.

"Yes?" I asked, my hand still on the door handle.

The cat's tail swished. "Thank you."

I had no idea why she was thanking me, but I nodded. "Of course."

Belladonna hopped out of the cubby back up to the second level and closed her eyes. I took a deep, loud breath, let it out slowly, and reluctantly left Belladonna to continue her mourning.

Chapter Ten

"WELL, THAT'S ONE HECK OF A STORY, ELLIE." DR. Laurie Gray's eyes were sharp and piercing behind her bifocals as she listened to my story. Her expression was thoughtful as she leaned away from the table. "Anything is possible, I suppose. A magical dish—"

"Tray—"

"Whatever." Tablerock's premiere veterinarian looked at me with a mixture of disbelief and wonder. "A magical object that glows on its own and seems to broadcast words that may—or may not—come from the cat sitting on it. If true, do you have any idea how useful that would be in my practice? If not true, frankly, you may call up a demon or something. Get a priest over there to bless the place."

"I'm not Catholic."

"I don't think it matters." Laurie grabbed a corn chip and plunged it into the spicy queso we'd ordered. "Let me ask you this. How do you know it's not a hallucination? Is the thing really talking? Really glowing?" She popped the chip in her mouth and bit down with a crunch.

I felt my cheeks flushing with irritation, and I was taken aback by the suggestion I was out of my mind. "You're kidding, right?"

Laurie looks bewildered. "No, I'm serious. Maybe you're just under stress. Are you still having problems with the payments on the—"

"I'm not stressed," I said defensively, cutting her off. I took a sip of my sweet tea, trying to swallow my pride, but it kept coming back up like bile. "Sorry. Yes, maybe I'm a little under stress, but it's not like that's abnormal. Non-profit animal work is not exactly a get-rich-quick scheme."

"Of course not."

"But Evie heard it, too. It's real, Laurie. Or at least it seems real. I don't know why Fiona Blackwell sent it to me before she got whacked in the middle of downtown, but she sent it to me and I have no idea what to do with it now."

A confused look flashed across Laurie's face. "What do you mean, what do you do with it?" she said, waving her hand as if brushing my concern aside. "I think you're being a little too cautious with this thing. Use it to talk to Fiona's cat, Ellie. Why on earth wouldn't you? The cat probably knows as much as Fiona did." Laurie lifted an eyebrow and tilted her head. "Maybe more."

The waiter, a youthful young man, arrived with a platter stacked with sizzling plates of fajitas, rice, and refried beans. He set the plates down carefully, grinning broadly at us while he displayed the gold tooth in his left front incisor. "Anything else I can bring you, ladies?"

The pungent aroma of sour cream and cheese filled the air as Laurie piled more toppings onto her fajita. "No, I think we're good for now. But thanks," I told him.

Laurie glanced up and nodded.

With a quick nod and a sly wink at Laurie, the waiter walked away to attend to another table.

"Well, now," she said, tossing her shoulder-length hair.

"Oh, please. That waiter is young enough to be your kid."

"He is young enough to be my kid. But he's not my kid, right?" She took a bite, chewed, and swallowed. "Anyway, back to the magic disk thing. Just ask Belladonna. She was Fiona's cat, after all. Most people's cats are an ever present focus of their lives. She may not know everything Fiona knew, but I bet she knows an awful lot."

"I don't want to traumatize her." I picked at the strips of beef on my fajita listlessly while Laurie eagerly devoured her food. "The cat's barely eating and sleeps all the time. If she was a person, I wouldn't go poke her in the middle of her grief and go 'Hey, I know the person closest to you in the world just croaked, but could I get some help here?'" I popped a jalapeño popper in my mouth. "She needs to come out of it in her own time."

"She is a person. A cat person, but a person. As much of a person as you or me. And let me ask you this—what if someone killed Fiona to get the talking cat circle thing?" She left the question unanswered, hanging in the air. "You said Mayor Wannabe already showed up at your shelter demanding Belladonna. In mourning or not, that cat could be in danger." Her face animated as she gestured, her eyes wide with emotion even as she dropped her voice's volume. "If the bloviator in sparkle-boots is going after the talking tray, she's going to go through the cat to get it. And that's if she does it the legal way."

I chuckled softly, taking a slow sip of my sweet tea as I listened to the ice clanking in my glass. I noticed her arched eyebrows as she gave me a quizzical look, and I quirked an eyebrow in response. "Mayor Wannabee?" I asked. "Who does Mayor Winthrop want to be?"

"Oh, please. Can't you tell? That woman is the worst Ann Richards impersonator I've ever seen. She's so full of herself and so power hungry, it makes my teeth hurt." Laurie shuttered. "That, and her poodle is so fat, the poor thing looks like a balloon animal." She glanced at my barely half-eaten fajita. "You need to eat, woman."

"I'm over two hundred pounds. Technically, I don't. My body can most likely meet the majority of my calorie requirements from stored fat."

"Oh, stop it."

"Did you know a person can survive up to a hundred and ten additional days for every fifty pounds of excess body fat? I figure cheesecake alone bought me an extra year if I land on a deserted island."

Laurie rolled her eyes. "Speaking of, beefcake—"

"Cheesecake—"

"I heard you doctored up town almost-hero Landon Rogers the other day." Her eyes sparkled with amusement as she playfully teased me. "Did he make any progress convincing you to go out with him?"

"No. I keep telling you and you keep not hearing me." I leaned back in the booth and pushed my plate away. "I'm at the shelter every day. I'm running Evie all over Austin for her doctor's appointments, and I spend every month bordering on bankruptcy because there aren't enough donations to supplement what the state pays us. I have enough stress to last a lifetime. I don't need more in the form of a romantic relationship. I'm done with those."

"Hey." Laurie's hand appeared soft and firm as it rested on my arm. She looked at me with concern, her eyes suddenly filled with worry. "Take a deep breath. I know things are getting financially tight, but I can help. If you'd let me donate—"

"Stop it. You do enough by giving the cats free vet care. You're not donating cash, too." I held up my hand. "I have no interest in dating anyone right now. Not Landon. Not anyone."

"Ellie, you're the closest thing I've ever had to a

sister, and I love you like I love my flesh and blood," Laurie said, her tone showing there was a but coming.

"But?"

Laurie looked frustrated, her face flushed as she slammed her hand down on the table. Her outburst startled the waiter, causing him to trip over a chair and land with a loud thud. "But you are a total prude. Your life could be so much more exciting if you'd just get out there a little. There's more to life than your kid and your cats."

Harsh.

"You're the greatest example of a liberated woman making full use of her freedom I've ever seen, right? I should be more like you?" My tone was more judgmental than I'd intended, tinged with an underlying sense of frustration—Laurie hadn't been on a date any more recently than I had. She just talked a better game.

Laurie looked unfazed. "Well, ouch."

"Yeah, sorry. I'm just tired." I glanced at my FitWatch. The time magically displayed. "As much as I'd love to continue arguing about this, it's almost nine. I have to get back—Matt's leaving in a few minutes and I need to be at the house."

Laurie nodded, instantly understanding. "I got it. Look, about the cat tray thing?" She plucked a slice of beef off my plate and popped it in her mouth. "You don't have to figure out everything right now. Just take things a step at a time. You do, though, have to take a step. Talk to Belladonna. Just treat her like any other person who just lost their caretaker. Trust me." Laurie's face scrunched seriously. "Cats are some of the most resilient animals there are."

I drove home from dinner that evening feeling conflicted. Laurie's words had stirred up a storm of emotions within me, making me question whether I could keep all the balls I was juggling in the air.

"Dating," I snorted, whispering to myself. "She's out of her mind."

With all the challenges I faced daily—the lack of adequate funding, the never-ending demands on my time by the cats, courts, and police, plus Evie's issues—I reminded myself I was doing my best.

Even if I did sometimes hate doing it alone.

Despite Laurie's teasing, I also knew that she cared deeply about me and wanted nothing more than to see me happy and fulfilled in every aspect of my life. And she was right about Belladonna and that psychic glowy table thing. With a newfound sense of resolve, I drove home determined to put Laurie's words into action.

I would start by reaching out to Belladonna, who needed my help now more than ever before, and try to ease her suffering. No matter what it took.

Well, tomorrow.

I'd do it tomorrow.

As I went to pull into my driveway, I had to swerve

late to avoid a car parked on the side of the road, its headlights off. It was a newer model sedan, its blue paint gleaming in the moonlight. There were no bumper stickers or other markings that would give me a clue who might be inside.

I slowed as I passed the car, trying to get a look at the driver. The windows were tinted, making it difficult to see inside. I could make out a figure in the driver's seat, but couldn't tell if it was a man or a woman.

Darn it. I didn't look at the license plate.

As I pulled into my driveway and got out of my car, I kept my eye on the sedan and debated whether I should pull back out to see what the license plate was. I waited a few moments, watching, but there was no sign of movement from the other vehicle.

Someone's probably parked there to rest, I told myself.

As I walked up the walkway to my front door, I shrugged off my unease, telling myself I was being paranoid.

But when I cast one last glance at the mystery car, it lurched into motion.

Its engine roared as it pulled away from the curb and zoomed off down the road, the headlights flaring like twin beacons as the vehicle sped up. The car's tires screeched as it took a corner and vanished into the night.

Chapter Eleven

I MADE MY WAY INTO THE HOUSE AND WAS GREETED by Evie and Matt laughing hysterically at a television show. "I'm home," I said, hanging the keys on the wall and setting my purse on the entry table. "Laurie says hello, by the way."

"Hey, Mom!"

"I'm just going to watch the end of this episode if that's okay, Ms. Rockwell," Matt called, and then he laughed once more.

"Sure, that's fine, Matt."

Peeking into the living room from the doorway, I was momentarily struck by the absurdity of the scene before me.

The living room was filled with a jumble of bodies and furniture.

Matt's feet were hanging off one end of the couch,

while Evie took up most of the other side. Multiple cats sat at various points on both the couch and the kids, their soft fur and inquisitive eyes visible in the dim light. A sea of even more shelter cats were sprawled at various relaxed stages on the surrounding floor.

Smiling, I headed toward the kitchen to put my leftovers in the fridge.

Matt and Evie were good friends.

A happy accident I hadn't planned on when Matthew Alfonso Garcia showed up four years ago with a volunteer application in one hand and a Starbucks coffee in the other.

We'd barely settled fully in Tablerock, the shelter finally open after a year of painstaking work, when Matt and Darla arrived within days of one another. The three-bedroom, two-story main house—my shelter's only home for the first year—was so far out on the outskirts of town it was almost in the next one.

I didn't accept them as volunteers hoping they'd—

The sound of shattering glass pierced through the air, followed by a sharp gasp from Evie.

"Ms. Rockwell!" The sharp edge of Matt's voice was harsh and panicked. "Evie's dropped her glass and..." Suddenly, he trailed off, struggling to gauge Evie's condition and find the right words to describe it. "Anyway, if you could bring a bandage with you when you come, that'd be great."

"I'll be right there," I said, grabbing the bandages and

heading back toward the living room. The glass, a gift Evie had brought back from a camp for dealing with heart disease, was shattered on the dark wood floor, its contents soaking into the weave of a jute accent rug. "Oh, what a shame. You got that at camp when you—"

"I—I—I can't—" Evie's face was twisted in a grimace, as she panted rapidly.

"Yes, you can," I told her. "Just breathe, honey. Count, and breathe."

Her hand trembled as it pointed toward the shattered cup, and her other hand slapped her thigh to vent the frustration she couldn't verbalize. "It—I—It—" Evie looked up at me, her face contorted with anger and frustration.

"Hey, it's okay, Evie. Just breathe. Slowly, just breathe," Matt said, his voice soothing. "We've got this. The sei—" He glanced at me, his eyes clouded with concern as he stopped himself. "Sorry." Matt smiled at Evie. "It'll pass in just a minute. Just breathe deep."

Matt still had a hard time not calling them seizures, but I'd made him stop. That wasn't what they were. It wasn't what the doctors called them, and it wasn't what they were.

Actually, the doctors didn't call them anything specific, either.

They were like panic attacks, but more...complicated than that.

When Evie hit a higher order function—like reasoning, decision-making, constructing a sentence, doing math—that she couldn't do, it surprised and frustrated her. Her frustration would lead to panic, and her panic would enrage her. All of this swirling within could over-whelm her.

"Give me your hand, sweetheart," I told her gently, holding my hand out. If I could get her to focus on doing one thing, one small thing, it could anchor her to the mental exit ramp. "Give me your hand so I can bandage it."

She stared at me, furious.

That was okay.

Evie may become engulfed in the overwhelming emotion even as she desperately searches for the solution she couldn't quite see. The more she tried and failed to find a solution, the more emotional she became, and the more she spiraled—until she froze, unable to speak, move, or get herself out of it.

But if she got control of one thing—just one thing—it was like the first rung on a ladder that would lead her up and out of the darkness.

"Evie," I said. "Lift your hand and place it in mine."

Her hand twitched. Twice. Three times.

"Come on, sweetheart, you can do it."

Her slender fingers twitched as she struggled to free herself from the immobilizing panic. Finally, Evie's arm flew upward and her hand landed in my hand.

"Good girl," I whispered.

The second the bandage was in place, Evie pushed

away from me and scrambled off the couch, dropping to the floor and scooping up the broken glass.

"Thanks," she muttered. "I got it."

She appeared to be her old self again, with clear thoughts and a sense of shame over what had happened. Her movements were frantic and quick, her eyes downcast. I could tell she was embarrassed by what had happened.

Matt moved to help. "Evie, don't, let me get—"

She answered him with a soft, "I said I've got it."

He was so good with her, so patient, so sweet. "She's got it, Matt. Evie's fine," I assured him.

"Yeah. Yeah, okay." He scrubbed his hands through his russet-colored hair, trying to calm himself down, trying to fight the urge to swoop in and do it for her.

I knew it was hard.

It was hard not to jump in and want to do everything for her, to make it easier for her.

I'd been there.

In some ways, I always would be.

"I'll get the broom," Matt said.

"No. No broom." A shard of Evie's former favorite cup scraped the wood floor as she dragged it across. "I've got it. I said I've got it." Her voice was harder, more determined as she looked around the living room, searching for other pieces. "Just let me clean up the damn thing, will you?"

"I'm sorry," he said, his tone low, apologetic. "I was only trying to help."

"Don't apologize, either," she said, her voice strained. Evie's shoulders were tense and rigid as she stared intently at the kind young man. "None of this has anything to do with you, Matt. Not a thing."

Matt's expression seemed to wish it were otherwise.

I tossed and turned in bed that night, my mind overwhelmed with everything in my life. My mind was active, racing, whirling, and it churned up question after question, but no solutions.

How could I convince Evie she could date someone and trust someone?

What if someone killed Fiona to get at the plate-tray thing I had sitting in my house?

How on earth did Fiona get out of jail? Did someone pay for her bail?

And the murders of Fiona and Beau. They had to be connected somehow, didn't they?

I thought back to the day that Evie and I moved to Tablerock. At that moment, it had felt like everything was possible, like there was nothing we couldn't overcome. I mean, how many people take a corporate severance package and gamble it all on opening up a nonprofit cat rescue? We'd built it from the ground up, too, with plenty of space to grow and flourish.

As the years went by, Tablerock eventually felt like home.

But now it just felt like everything was spinning out of control—and the small town we sought to create a refuge in (for us and the cats) now had two murders and a Wal-Mart on the way.

Ugh.

I threw the covers off me.

Laurie was right.

I needed to take things one step at a time, and the first step was to talk to Belladonna. I could do nothing about the Wal-Mart, the toll road the county was building, or Evie's inability to see that Matt was perfect for her.

But I could go talk to that cat.

The wood floors were cold under my bare feet, and I felt a chill run down my spine as I made my way down the corridor toward the isolation room. I was about to open the door when I decided against it. I softly knocked and then called for her.

"Belladonna?" I whispered. "Can I come in?"

Belladonna meowed loudly.

"That's 'yes,' right?" I asked.

There was no response, so I took a deep breath and opened the door.

Belladonna was in the far corner, facing the wall, when I entered. She turned her head and looked at me, her expression the same mournful one she'd had since I told her about Fiona's death.

I knelt down and petted her.

She responded by turning away. Her body tensed and she hissed softly.

"I understand," I whispered.

She turned back to me with a cautious eye, as if she didn't quite believe me.

"I know you're tired, Belladonna, and you probably want to sleep until the pain of losing your mom goes away. I can't say that I blame you. What happened to Fiona and Beau was—"

At the mention of Beau's name, Belladonna jumped up, her back arched and her ears pressed back. She hissed once menacingly.

"What's the matter? What did I say?"

The black cat's eyes narrowed as she let out a sinister growl, exposing sharp teeth. It sounded like the rumbling of thunder.

"Okay, okay." I raised my hands, trying to calm the agitated cat. "I didn't mean to upset you. I'm just trying to say that it's—"

Belladonna leaped into action, her long legs propelling her like a newborn gazelle. She jumped onto the cat tree and turned to face me, her yellow eyes blazing with rage. She hissed once more before leaping to the second level, where the magical disk erupted in light the moment her front paws touched it.

"Don't you dare mention his name to me!" Belladonna's voice was forceful and fierce as a lioness. "Fiona died because of him! I don't want to talk about him.

Ever!" A long, low hiss came out of her mouth as if she were purging herself of something dark from the depths of her soul. "That man is roasting in a spit in the deepest pits of hell if your human afterlife has any justice."

Belladonna's hatred for Beau wasn't surprising given what I knew about Fiona and Beau's marriage—or, more accurately, the rumors about Fiona and Beau's marriage. What struck me as curious was the cat's assumption that Fiona was dead because of him.

"Bella, Fiona wanted me to help clear her name," I told the cat as I sat down in front of the glowing cubbyhole, tucking my legs beneath my nightgown. "Did you know that? When I went to see her in prison, she told me—"

"Did she ask about me?" The cat's tone was angry as she paced in the tiny carpeted shelter. "Did Fiona ask how I was? If I missed her? Did she tell you what a toad her husband was, staying married to her for the money even though he lived with that stupid bimbo mayor?" Belladonna asked me, her eyes flashing. "Did she tell you that despicable fool broke in to her house the day before he died and held me down on this stupid plate to show that horrible Winthrop woman how it—"

That got my attention. "Wait a minute. Beau did what now?"

Belladonna came to a dead halt and stared at me coldly. "Are you hard of hearing?"

"No, I just wanted to make sure I heard you—"

"Just stop talking." She lifted her tail and sat down,

prim and proper as an English lady at tea. "I forgot you humans were slow."

I raised my eyebrows. "Belladonna, I—"

"The day before Beau Blackwell died, he came into Wardwell Manor dragging that debased cheap floozie behind him. That horrid harlot seized me from my lofty vantage on the library window perch and unceremoniously dropped my poor body onto the etched mirror with a callous disregard for my endangered venerable age." The cat hissed again. "Obviously, I hurled a string of unseemly words at the churlish scoundrel."

Belladonna sounded like she was reading off a script for a period drama.

"How do you know what day Beau died?" I asked. "Not even the police are sure, since his body was dumped."

"Twice now, I have told you this. If your faculties are insufficient to comprehend my words, that is no fault of mine." She hissed at me. "And I told you—I don't want to talk about him."

"Fine," I said, taking deep breaths to keep her from realizing how infuriated she was making me. Belladonna was volatile, dramatic, condescending, and frustrating— in other words, she was a cat. I also didn't remember her telling me anything of the sort, but she clearly had no intention of answering my question. "You stated Fiona died because of him. Why do you believe that?"

"I do not believe it, I know it."

"Okay, what do you know that makes you think that?"

Belladonna shot to her feet. "I am weary of talking."

I was weary of translating the cat's speech from fake Victorian to modern day English, but I was trudging on with this. And I hadn't slept all day.

"Belladonna, please." I sounded a little desperate, but I didn't care. "You need to tell me what you know."

Belladonna wrapped her tail around her front paws and sat down. "We'll discuss the matter after the solicitor calls on you. Has he done so yet?"

"The solicitor." I blinked. "You mean a lawyer? No. What lawyer?"

"You must parlay with the lawyer first. After that colloquy, you will have far more information than you do now."

"Belladonna, why do I need to see a lawyer? And could you answer me in English as opposed to whatever the hell it is you're talking in?"

The cat glared at me. "The will."

I stared at the cat. "The will."

"Yes, the will. Now there will be no further discussion of the matter until the lawyer is here. I shall see you tomorrow." Belladonna shuffled out of the cubbyhole.

I sighed. I had a feeling that whatever Belladonna knew was vitally important, but she clearly would not tell me until I talked to this mysterious lawyer.

I turned around and trudged back up to bed, grumbling to myself as I lay back down and pulled the covers up over my head.

Whatever was happening, I knew this strange and mysterious cat was at the center of it all. And if I wanted to figure out what she knew, I had to talk to that lawyer as soon as possible.

Too bad I had no idea what lawyer she was talking about.

Chapter Twelve

THE NEXT MORNING, A GENTLE RAIN TAPPING ON the window woke me up. I frowned at the four a.m. alarm clock staring back at me.

I was used to waking up early, but not at this hour.

I wasn't upset about staying in bed. My mind was a little foggy, tired from the previous few days' stress. That, and that I hadn't had a full night's sleep since Fiona was arrested and Belladonna arrived. As the rain pattered on the window, I closed my eyes once more.

The sound of the phone ringing jolted me awake. I grunted as I looked at the clock. It was just after six o'clock in the morning. I rubbed my cheek with my hand, trying to clear the fog from my eyes, and frowned as I focused on the caller ID.

LAW OFFICE

"Hello?" I asked, still half asleep.

"Good morning! I sincerely apologize for the early

morning hour, but it's imperative I get a hold of Eleanor Rockwell. Are you Eleanor Rockwell?" an overly perky voice asked me.

"Yes, that's me." I yawned. "Who are you again?"

"Oh, I didn't say. But this is Carol Jones. I'm a paralegal at the Law Offices of Slater, Slater & Johanson over in Woodville," she responded in a clipped, fully caffeinated voice.

I roused myself and sat up. "Yes, ma'am. What can I help you with?"

"I apologize for calling you so early, but I just learned that the reading of Fiona Blackwell's will is going to take place at nine this morning, and no one called you to invite you to attend. I can't imagine how that got overlooked." I heard shuffling papers. "Mrs. Blackwell was adamant that she wanted a will reading 'like they had in the old days,' although reading a will is obsolete now, you know." Carol sighed. "She was an interesting woman."

"She was at that," I agreed, and then yawned. "Why do I need to be there? If there's information about Belladonna, your office can just send me a certified copy of whatever we need to know here at the shelter."

"Well, yes, I could do that, but Mrs. Blackwell was very specific regarding who was to be present when her will was read aloud," the paralegal explained. "You were among the individuals she specified. Again, I apologize for calling so early, but I was on vacation and will read-

ings are no longer being performed, so the other parale-
gals had no clue this needed to be done."

"Who else did she want there?" I asked.

"Well, now, she didn't have any children with
Beau," Carol said, and I heard more paper shuffling.
"So there are no children. But she wanted Jessa
Winthrop to attend, as well as Azalea Jones, her maid.
No relation." More shuffling. "Oh, and Waldo
Monroe."

I frowned. "The old guy that teaches martial arts in
the park?"

"He's sixty-one," Carol said in a disapproving tone,
as if I had insulted her grandfather. "Anyway, can you
make it?" she asked. "Again, I really apologize for calling
so early, but I doubt you would have received the
message on time if I had waited until nine o'clock."

Why on earth is Jessa Winthrop going to be there?

Facing off against the demanding mayor once more
wasn't high on my list of things to do early in the morning, and considering how Fiona felt about Jessa, I didn't
think there was a snowball's chance in hell she left
Belladonna to the mayor.

"Do you know why the mayor will be there?
Considering their history, I can't believe Fiona would
leave that woman anything."

"I have no idea, but I have to admit I'm pretty
curious myself," she said with a chuckle. She paused.
"Would you like to speak to Mr. Johanson? He's the one
who's looked over the will. Maybe he'll tell you."

"No, that's okay." I glanced at the clock. "I'll be there."

"Oh. Okay, then," Carol said, sounding disappointed. "I'll let Mr. Johanson know. Again, I'm sorry for the early morning call."

"It's no problem," I said, hanging up the phone.

I leaned back against the pillows and stared at the ceiling, my mind racing. What could Fiona possibly have left for Jessa Winthrop? And why was Waldo Monroe in the will reading? He didn't seem like the type of person Fiona would have been close to.

I got out of bed and got ready for the day, my mind still racing with questions.

Jessa Winthrop was the first person I saw. Her platinum hair was pulled back into a tight bun and her black suit fit like a glove, showing off the curves of her lean body. She appeared to be dressed for a dignitary's funeral, with flawless hair and makeup, giving her a polished and put-together appearance.

"What are you doing here?" she asked me, her expression stern. "And how did you know where to go?"

GPS on my phone like everyone else?

"The office called me," I told her. "I didn't know Fiona was going to have a will reading I needed to attend until this morning. The paralegal got me at the crack of dawn."

"Fiona had a lot of unique things," Jessa replied with a hint of a smile. "The will reading drama is just one of them, I suppose." She looked me up and down. "You didn't even know Fiona. I have no idea why you'd be invited here."

I opened my mouth—

Then I closed it.

I was about to remind her that Fiona didn't know who I was, but Fiona despised her. But then I remembered I didn't know these people, and I had no idea what was going on with Jessa's attendance, Fiona's will, or the magical item stashed in my house.

And until I did, it was better to watch and wait.

And keep my lips zipped.

The door to the office squeaked open and Landon's grizzled martial arts instructor, Waldo Monroe, shuffled in. He may be in his sixties, but with his salt and pepper hair and dark gray goatee, he could pass for a man in his forties in any club or bar. Waldo was dressed simply in a black suit and bore more than a passing resemblance to the actor Sam Elliot from the film Roadhouse.

I looked down at my pale pink Capri pants and white shirt (with a charming picture of a kitten in a cowboy hat.) I pulled uncomfortably at the bottom of the shelter staff green hoodie I wore over my outfit and wondered if I should have dolled myself up. Considering the two mournful fashionistas in the waiting room with me, I felt under dressed.

"Good morning!" Carol singsonged. The perky paralegal glided into the waiting room, her dress a splash of vibrant pink against the muted tones of the office setting. She greeted us all with a warm smile and a formal handshake. "My name's Carol Jones, and I see everyone's here. Can I get anyone anything to drink? Coffee, tea, water? Maybe something stronger?"

We all shook our heads.

"Wonderful. If you'll follow me, we can get started."

"What about Azalea?" I asked. "I thought she was coming?"

Jessa Winthrop twisted her head at the sound of the name. "How do you know about Azalea Jones?"

"Ms. Jones told me her name." I pointed. "I asked who was coming."

"She won't be joining us." Carol said nothing more about why the maid skipped her employer's dramatically cast old-fashioned will reading. "Everyone ready?"

She led us into the conference room, where a middle-aged man sat at the head of a large mahogany table. He wore wire-rimmed glasses and had thinning blond hair.

We entered quietly and took our seats around the large meeting table. Jessa sat down near the man and I sat next to Jessa, while Waldo sat across from us. Carol placed a stack of papers in front of the man at the head of the table and then stood back, hovering.

I switched off my phone.

"Thank you for coming," the spectacled man said. "I am Charles Johanson, the executor of Fiona Blackwell's will. Per the deceased's instructions, I will read the will today." The lawyer looked nervously at Jessa Winthrop. "Since we're all here, let's get to it." He took a deep breath and read. "I, Fiona Blackwell, being of sound mind and body—"

"No, no. No, thank you, Charlie," Jessa replied, cutting him off with a shake of her head.

Charlie?

The attorney looked up.

"I'd like to get this over with as soon as possible. Just give us the crux of it. You look like you're holding about thirty pages, and I'm not sitting here listening to you read all that." The mayor's voice dripped with the arrogance of a woman used to getting her own way. "Just tell us what we need to know."

"Someplace to be, Mayor Winthrop?" Waldo asked in a raspy voice.

"Oh, please, Waldo. Just call me Mayor," she responded with a dismissive wave of her hand. "I just don't see the point in dragging this out. I have a city to run."

"Technically, it's a town," I murmured.

"We appreciate your dedication to duty, Jessa," Waldo replied with a forced smile.

Jessa Winthrop leaned back in her chair with a smirk on her face. "Don't be so smug, Monroe. Running a business on public property? That's not exactly allowed, is it?" she asked.

Waldo leaned forward, his eyes narrowed in anger.

"I'd hate to see the town lose you as a resource."

"I bet you would," he responded.

"Would I lie?" she asked, and fluttered her eyelashes.

The tension and hostility in the room was increasing with each passing second, but I had no idea where it specifically came from. My head swiveled back and forth between Jessa and Waldo as they seethed with low-key passive-aggression.

Waldo jammed his finger on the table. "Is that a threat, Mayor Win—"

"If we could just get back to the matter at hand," the lawyer interrupted.

"I think we'd all like to get this over with as soon as possible," I added, agreeing with the mayor. "Maybe we should all just let him read and hold our comments to the end?"

"Oh, you think so, do you?" Mayor Winthrop's face turned an alarming shade of red. "I don't recall anyone asking for your opinion, but now that you've spoken up, where do you have to be?"

Nowhere, really.

Remarkably saucy response, I noted.

After all, I'd agreed with her.

Waldo and Jessa did not like each other, and I didn't want to be caught in the middle of whatever was bubbling up between the two. Speeding this up seemed like a good idea.

I didn't respond.

"Unless there are any objections, I'll just get to it,"

he said with a weary voice. "To summarize, Mrs. Blackwell has left most of her estate to the Silver Circle Cat Rescue."

It was like a bomb dropped in the office, leaving everyone stunned.

After about ten seconds, Waldo let out a low chuckle.

Jessa sat up straighter in her chair, an angry look on her face. "What?" she asked Johanson incredulously. "Beau promised! Fiona never even mentioned her, and Beau certainly never said a word! I don't believe it! That cat and all of its stuff is supposed to go to—"

"Mayor," the lawyer said. He gave Jessa a look of warning. "Get a hold of yourself."

Her mouth snapped shut, but her cheeks stayed pinkish red.

"Wouldn't want to say something you shouldn't, huh, Mayor?" Waldo asked her quietly.

"Shut up, Monroe," the mayor growled.

Everyone else in the room seemed to understand the subtext except me.

"I don't understand," I said.

And that may have been the understatement of the year.

"Ms. Rockwell, 90 percent of the Blackwell assets have been placed into a legacy gift to your nonprofit," the lawyer told me. "This is, however, a restricted gift. It's conditional upon your nonprofit maintaining and caring for the cat known as Belladonna—and all that cat's possessions—for the rest of her feline life. Do you understand?" Stunned, I nodded. "Once the cat passes naturally, the gift becomes unrestricted. Your organization can do with it whatever it wants."

"And does Ms. Rockwell know how much that gift is?" Waldo prodded the lawyer. "Have y'all reached out and let her know?" He stared across the table at the mayor. "You should tell her."

The lawyer cleared his throat before replying. "The bequest is for twenty-seven million dollars. Give or take. As well as ownership and control of Wardwell Manor."

I gasped audibly.

Jessa's eyes nearly popped out of her head, and Waldo let out a low whistle.

"Congratulations, Ms. Rockwell," Carol Jones told me, her eyes twinkling.

I sat there in shock, trying to process what the lawyer had said.

Twenty-seven million dollars was more money than I could even wrap my head around. It would ensure that Silver Circle could keep rescuing cats for years to come.

I could hire Darla and Matt.

I could build on to the property.

Or I could move the shelter to Wardwell Manor, where there was a ton of room.

I could pay off the stupid van note.

It was a miraculous amount of money to see. More than anyone I knew had ever seen, no matter what successes we might have achieved in our lives.

It was shocking.

It was humbling.

It didn't seem real.

"I—I don't know what to say," I stammered, still in disbelief.

"Well, congratulations, Ms. Rockwell," Jessa said through gritted teeth. "It seems like you've hit the jackpot through absolutely no effort of your own." She glared at me, her eyes filled with resentment and anger.

Despite her jealousy and bitterness, I refused to let her get to me. Instead, I simply ignored her insults as I tried to process my good fortune.

"As happy as I am for Ms. Rockwell's cats, why are the mayor and I here?" Waldo asked, suspicion etched into his features. "Did Fiona say anything about us, or leave us something?" He tilted his head. "Not that I care, mind you. I'm just not sure what we're here for."

I sat back in my chair, still trying to wrap my head around the news.

The lawyer nodded. "She did not want your inheritance to be read aloud until you looked at it, but here is the paper that outlines what she left you." Johanson slid a thick sheet across the table. Waldo reached out, picked it up, and frowned as he skimmed through it. Then he smiled. Then he chuckled and glanced up at Jessa.

"What?"

"Fiona left me a gigantic pile of money."

"How much?" Jessa asked, her voice laced with jealous venom.

The humor faded from Waldo's face, and he looked back down at the paper. "Well, now, see, it's not so much the what as it is the why." He glanced up. "It's earmarked for a campaign. My campaign." He paused dramatically. "To defeat you."

Jessa snorted in disbelief. "You don't have enough money to defeat me! That pile would have to be enormous."

"It is."

She blinked. "Bring it on. This town loves me. You'll never beat me."

"Maybe," Waldo said. Then he shrugged. "Believe what you want, Jessa. But I think Fiona realized she should have taken you on a long time ago." He leaned back in his chair and grinned at her smugly. "You and Beau got away with too much—"

Jessa Winthrop seethed with fury. "How would you know?"

"You realize Fiona and I had a relationship, right?"

"What?" Jessa yelped, lunging for the paper.

Waldo held it up out of her reach and scanned it again before handing it over.

As Jessa read the paper, her face turned redder and redder until she finally crumpled it up into a ball and threw it across the room.

"And that was the reason she wanted you here, Mayor," Carol told Mayor Winthrop with a saccharine sweet smile. "She wanted you to know that she was taking you on from beyond the grave, I believe. She wanted you to see it."

"See what?"

The paralegal stared at the paper in her hand. "All of it fall apart."

"You absolute b—," Jessa stopped herself even though she was visibly fuming. "I'll get you for this. You got me in here just to humiliate me."

"That's just what I've always admired about you, Jessa," Waldo told her. "You've always clued in so quickly."

"You shut the hell up, Waldo Monroe," she told him, leaping to her feet. "You know nothing about anything. Fiona was just jealous that Beau loved me and not her. Despite all her money, she still couldn't keep him."

"She wanted nothing back you took from her," Waldo said.

"If you and that old prune had a relationship, well, that won't do anything but make you look bad, will it? Maybe you killed her! Or you," Jessa turned and stared at me. "I know you went to see her. Maybe all this is your doing!"

She stormed out of the office, leaving Waldo and me sitting at the table.

"I'm sorry about that," Johanson said after a long moment of silence. "I suspected Mayor Winthrop was going to be a bit...annoyed at the reading," he admitted after searching for the appropriate word. "I didn't think the situation was going to devolve as much as it did."

The expression on the lawyer's face implied he knew exactly how upset the mayor would be, and it was less of an outburst than he'd prepared for.

I nodded, still trying to process everything that had happened.

It seemed surreal that Fiona Blackwell had left such a large sum of money to the nonprofit to ensure that her cat was cared for from beyond the grave. I'd had no hint that she'd done that. None.

Yet Belladonna knew.

"Well," Waldo Monroe said as he stood up, "I should be going. I'll let myself out." He looked down at me. "I'd love to come by and see Belladonna, if I could. She may be the only other being on the planet that loved Fiona as much as I did."

I nodded, still feeling dazed. "Sure. That would be fine."

And with that, Waldo Monroe left the office, leaving me alone with the lawyer, the paralegal, and a pile of questions so high I didn't think I'd ever answer them all.

Chapter Thirteen

I sat on a well-worn bench in the park, gazing out over the peaceful waters of Lake Wildebridge, and tried to collect my thoughts after the shocking turn of events. As I breathed in the sweet scent of flowers, I tried to focus my thoughts on what lay ahead.

I took a deep breath just as Zora Hilliard power walked by with a huff and a nod. I smiled at her—but when I looked away, I heard her whisper, "It's her, Annie." A pause. "Well, she's here, just staring off into space. Probably feels like a truck hit her, poor thing." I looked back and saw her lips curled into a condescending smirk. "Yes, a very expensive truck. Of all the people to have that kind of luck. Can you believe it?"

Small towns.

I'd lay money on the fact that everyone had heard about the shelter's inheritance by this point. If I wasn't already the talk of the town, I was about to be.

"I thought I'd find you here." I looked up to find Landon hiking up the small hill toward the scenic bench. He walked with a purpose, and his expression held shades of concern. "How you holding up?" he asked when I didn't respond.

"Honestly?" I asked. "Worse than I thought when I left the lawyer's office." I looked up at Landon. I heaved a deep sigh. "Waldo called you, I take it?"

Landon gave a sharp nod.

I gestured toward the other side of the bench. "I didn't have an inkling that was coming, Landon. She said nothing to me the other day. To be honest, I don't know what Fiona was thinking."

"I think I might." He plopped down on the bench, pulled his cap off, and ran a hand through his hair. "By the way, Laurie called me, too."

My eyes narrowed.

My friend Laurie. Always plotting, always scheming. Even in this situation, Dr. Doolittle had to plot my romantic life.

Landon reached over and placed a comforting hand on my shoulder. "Do you want to talk about it?"

I raised an eyebrow as he glanced at me.

"You know, with the lawyers and all? I don't want to barrel into your private moment and force you to talk about it if you're not ready. If you are ready, though," he said, flashing a quick smile that caused his dimples to make an appearance, "I can listen if you need someone to talk to. I'm good at that."

I was about to say I was fine, that I didn't want to burden him with my problems, but the words got stuck in my throat. I looked at Landon and saw someone who was steady, someone who could handle anything I threw his way. And I realized maybe I needed someone to talk to.

And, you know, confiding in a guy that knew martial arts?

Maybe not such a bad thing in my situation.

"Actually," I said, "I think I would like that."

So I told him everything.

Maybe I shouldn't have.

But I did.

For the second time since telling my daughter not to run her mouth to anyone about the magical drink tray, I ran my mouth about the magical drink tray.

"My fear is that whatever got Beau and Fiona Blackwell killed might have just been willed to me with a demand that I take care of it for the rest of its life," I told him, my voice shaky.

Landon sat quietly and mulled over what he'd heard silently.

"And it's not just that, though that's the weirdest." I told him I was afraid I wouldn't manage such an astounding amount of money correctly, that I would waste this opportunity. That I had enough on my plate with taking care of Evie and running the shelter, that I didn't need the stress of this, too.

And as I talked, exposing the sudden fears that

gripped me, Landon listened patiently. He never interrupted me or tried to offer advice. He just let me vent my teapot turmoil steam until the pressure felt manageable again. "I think that's it."

"Yeah? Well, now." Landon nodded and leaned back on the bench, crossing his arms behind his head. "That is one heck of a tale, Ellie. Though I had heard tell of old Fiona having something like that, I can't say I ever believed it. And you say it's real? Huh. Will wonders never cease."

"I still can't believe it myself."

"Well, you seem to have a good handle on what's going on."

For a moment, I thought Landon was pulling my leg, but he looked at me with such earnestness in his eyes I knew he was serious. "I do?" I said.

"You do," he reassured me. "It sounds like you have a good head on your shoulders and are handling this mess as best you can. And if you need any advice or help along the way, I'm here for you, Ellie. So, what are you going to do from here? What's the first step?"

"What a simple question," I chuckled. I exhaled deeply and leaned back against the bench. "To be honest, I have no idea. I left Austin and corporate garbage in pursuit of a simpler, slower-paced life. A more authentic and kinder community for Evie and me. Simpler concerns. This?" I lifted my hands. "This is exactly the reverse of what I wanted."

He nodded sympathetically. "I can imagine."

"Can you?"

He chuckled. "Well, no. But I'm not that imaginative. I think maybe Fiona knew you could handle it. You're such a capable woman, Ellie. So was she. I think she saw that in you and she must have known you could handle anything," Landon said. "That's not necessarily a bad thing."

"No," I said, "I suppose it isn't."

"Sometimes the hardest choices are the ones that end up mattering the most."

"Are you a carpenter or a philosopher?" I asked with a sigh.

"No, ma'am. Just a country boy with too many years under his belt and too much time to think."

We sat there for a while longer, enjoying the peace of the park and each other's company. Something Landon said came back to me. "You knew about the talking tray before I said something?"

"Knew about it? Not really. Heard tell of it?" Landon shrugged. "Well, sure. Small towns always have their wild rumors and sordid gossip that may or may not be true. Everyone around these parts has heard of it once or twice. I thought nothing of that one until now, though."

"Ugh, rumors," I muttered.

"Well, Ellie, someone's always center stage in our local drama. The local paper needs something to write about."

He was right.

I sighed, remembering this week it would be me.

"I should probably get going," I said, getting to my feet. "Thank you for listening."

Landon stood as well and nodded. "I should probably get back to the office. But I'll follow you home first, just to make sure you get there safely."

"That's unnecessary," I protested.

"Nonsense. It's not about you. It's entirely selfish," he said. "I would feel better if I knew you got home safely. Now, you going to rob me of that, Ellie Rockwell?"

Landon Rogers was a southern gentleman personified.

From his faded denim jeans to his thick mane of salt and pepper hair, there was nothing about him that was not masculine. He was a place, a season, a way of life. Even from a distance, I could feel a warmth radiating off him, making me feel like I was standing too close to a very large and very warm fire.

I gave him a grateful smile.

Sure, he was being manipulative, taking advantage of an opportunity.

A little.

I knew it.

But even so, his care and concern made me blush. It wasn't often a semicentennial woman with a derriere the size of mine got to feel like a sixteen-year-old being courted to go steady. "All right. Thank you."

As we walked out of the park, he nodded and fell

into step beside me, the epitome of country charm. We were quiet for a while, lost in our own thoughts. Landon spoke up as we approached our cars, his work truck parked next to my—very expensive, recently unwisely financed—cat transport van.

"You know, Ellie, if you ever need to talk about anything, come find me. I might not have all the answers, but I promise to lend a listening ear. I'm here for you, Ellie. You know that, right? Whatever it is. I got your back."

I took a deep breath, held his gaze for a moment, and nodded. "I appreciate that, Landon. Thank you."

He nodded and climbed into his truck.

I kept an eye on him in my rear-view mirror as he followed me all the way back to the cat rescue, making sure I arrived safely. Although I suspected Landon had a hidden agenda, it was a thoughtful gesture for which I was grateful.

"Oh, this is not happening," I breathed as I turned onto my street.

Local news vans were parked in disorganized rows along the curb, their occupants eagerly waiting for something to happen. The media circus outside my house was a chaotic frenzy of movement as reporters jostled for position.

Why hadn't Evie called me?

I picked up my phone off the passenger seat and looked at it, cursing myself.

I didn't turn it back on after the attorney's office.

I drove quickly into the lot and pulled around near the back door, jumping out of my van with an umbrella despite the sky's utter absence of clouds. I opened it up and blocked the swarming reporters' view of me, but someone with a good vantage point spotted me.

"That's Eleanor! Eleanor Rockwell! Can we have a word with you?"

"No!" I shouted. "No comment. I have no comment!"

"The Independent here. What can you tell us about the cat shelter?"

"Eleanor! This way! Look here!"

The heavy, thudding steps of reporters running toward me reverberated through the air as they raced from the road to intercept me before I could reach the back door.

"Do you have any comment on the accusations being made against you?"

"Gazette here. What do you say to those who say you may have manipulated an old woman into giving you millions of dollars?"

The questions felt like they were coming at me from all sides.

I unlocked the door and stepped inside, slamming the outer door shut behind me. I leaned against it, heart pounding in my chest, and tried to calm myself down.

This was a nightmare. Pure and simple.

How had this even happened?

"I take it you spoke to the barrister?" a familiar feline voice bellowed from the isolation room. "I would assume that's why all these people are scurrying about in such a fashion on the lawn outside."

I narrowed my eyes and slammed the mantrap door behind me.

Bursting into the isolation room, I gave the black cat a withering stare. "Did you know about this?" Belladonna coiled at the top of the cat tree, her eyes alight with amusement as she watched me. "You said something about the lawyer. You had to know."

"Me?" she said, her tone like velvet. "Know what?"

"If you knew what Fiona did, why didn't you warn me, Belladonna?" I asked, coming to a stop in front of her. "I could have prepared for this pandemonium on my front lawn instead of hiding behind my umbrella!"

She stretched her sinewy body, the muscles rippling beneath her smooth, black fur. "It was your burden," she said matter-of-factly. "It was not for me to say. Besides, it was all tedious human information I do not care about. I should not have to delve into the minutiae of human experience—"

"Could you stop talking like an English butler?"

The cat's body quivered slightly as she took in my words. Her ears flicked back and forth in annoyance. "Fine. I wanted you to have time to think about what you were going to say to me. After all, you and I are going to be together for a very long time."

Belladonna regarded me for a moment before leaping down from her perch. She moved toward me, rubbing against my leg affectionately before looking up at me with her bright yellow eyes.

Ooh, cats are such manipulative sociopaths.

"You're twenty years old, Belladonna," I told the cat at my feet. "The average feline lifespan is twelve to eighteen years. I think you're overestimating your stamina."

She blinked and leaped back up to the cubby. As soon as it flared to life, her voice cracked toward me like a whip. "Hey, chubby, how about we race and we'll see who has stamina—"

"Hey!"

"Hey yourself. The rules say you can have the money if you take care of me until I die, woman." Belladonna's eyes narrowed. "If you think I can't run away from this budget hotel shelter to find someplace that shuttles me to the Four Seasons cat spa I deserve, you vastly underestimate my appetency for comfort."

Appetency?

Was that even a word?

So she did know.

"I will not turn this place into the Four Seasons of cat shelters," I said. "You're going to have to be content with this shelter, which is very efficient considering the little it's had to make do with. I live here, too, you know. It'll work just fine for you."

"Hmph," she said, turning her back on me haughtily. "We'll see about that."

As I stared at the black-furred back, I realized with a start that if Belladonna ran away, we'd not only lose the money, but it'd be a PR disaster (judging by the local news crews lining the front parking lot.)

Wow.

That manic cat knew what a barrel she had me bent over, and she would not give up her advantage.

Furry psycho.

Before I let my anger pull up a chair and settle in, I reminded myself that this was a cat who had just lost her home, her caregiver, and everything she knew.

Cats are naturally stoic—they are, after all, natural predators, which is why they instinctively hide signs of pain or vulnerability. Showing weakness in nature?

Excellent way to get eaten.

I also have to admit that what was mysterious and compelling in an animal with no words and no voice was maddening in an animal with opinions and speech to make them known.

"Fine," I said, throwing up my hands in defeat. "You have a point. We'll make some improvements. Some. We're not turning this into a cat spa. Some improvements. In exchange for a say over those improvements, promise you will not run away."

"I promise," she said, her voice dripping with honeyed innocence.

The cat stretched lazily once more and jumped

down from the cubby, padding over to me. She butted her head against my leg again and purred loudly.

"That no longer seems as adorable and sincere as it once did," I told her.

Belladonna's eyes widened and her ears flattened against her head in shock and disbelief. A low hiss escaped from between her clenched teeth, and then she turned and walked out of the isolation room.

Chapter Fourteen

I STOOD IN THE EMPTY ROOM AND STARED AT THE doorway.

"It's so quiet in here," I murmured. "So peaceful."

No one answered me.

I could hardly believe that just weeks ago, I was living life as usual, taking my second act in stride, determined to make it different—and more peaceful—than the first act of my rather complicated life. Had someone told me where I'd end up in a few short weeks, I would have scoffed at them in disbelief.

"That's what older people do, right?" I said and then laughed. "Scoff?"

Yep. I would have scoffed.

Yet there I was, at fifty years old—my second act dictated by my resentful, very pissed off cat.

The irony of it all was not lost on me.

Four years ago, I worked as a corporate manager in

one of the largest companies in the country. I had been with them for over ten years and had worked my way up to a high-level position. It was a great job—one that paid well and provided me with the stability I desired, so I could take care of myself and my family.

At first, it seemed like a dream come true. I had been promoted to the head of a department and felt like I was finally given the opportunity to make a real difference in the lives of those working for me—or so I thought.

Then the unthinkable happened.

Within a few years, I was asked to let go of all the people that worked for me, all the people I had grown close to—people who were like family to me. It felt like an impossible request; how could I possibly fire all these people?

How?

Because I had no choice. I didn't want someone they didn't know firing them. If it had to be someone, it had to be me.

So, I set out to meet with each person individually, one by one. I wanted to make sure that they knew it wasn't personal and that their dismissal had nothing to do with them or the work they had done for me. I also wanted them to know that I respected them deeply and was sorry for what had happened.

It was a grueling experience; not only was it emotionally draining, but it took an immense amount of time, too. In the end, I felt like I had done the right thing and showed each person the respect they deserved.

When they called me in to let me go, I knew it was coming. What use is a manager if there's no one left to manage?

But they were very careful with me. Maybe because I was over forty and had a disabled daughter, or maybe because of all the hard work I had put in over the years—whatever it was, they were gentle and made sure that I got a big severance package.

Oddly enough, I left the building with an immense sense of relief; relieved to put this chapter of my life behind me, relieved to finally start over, relieved to get away from the misery of watching everything my department built get torn down.

While I knew it would take some time to adjust, I had a newfound sense of hope that things would eventually get better. Little did I know that newfound hope would come as a cat—a terrified, gentle and loving cat.

My old boss had gotten me an interview with a large corporation moving its headquarters to Austin. They wanted me to run their customer service department. The perky woman at the outdoor table at the fancy restaurant—twenty years younger than me, if not more—had just finished telling me how much her company's considerable success depended upon the fabulous customer service people they had in New York.

"Would I need to travel back and forth between Austin and New York?" I asked between bites of a salad.

"No," she answered. "We'll be consolidating our customer service department here in Austin."

"Oh. So they'll be moving to Austin?"

"No, we'll be replacing them once we have operations up and running here."

I don't remember pushing away from the table and walking away from the perky woman with the plans to fire all the people that made her company special to save a few dollars, but that's what I did. Thanked her for the chance to meet her, that I appreciated her consideration, but that the job was not for me.

Instead of heading to my car, I wandered into a park close to the restaurant.

That's when I saw her.

A scrawny, bedraggled little thing curled up beneath a bush. She was so scared and alone, a baby of ten weeks, maybe twelve—and in desperate need of love and care. She stared at me with those big green eyes as if to say, "hey, why don't you help me out?"

Maybe it was that I could just scoop her up and help her, and that damage firing all those people had done to my psyche.

Maybe it was that no rich corporate jerk could tell me I couldn't help this kitten.

Maybe it was that I needed to do something with the rest of my life that didn't twist my soul into knots.

Whatever it was, I decided this was what I needed to do—start a cat rescue.

Yes, most people would have just taken the kitten home and adopted her.

And I did that.

But I also started a cat rescue.

Over the years, I've taken in cats of all shapes and sizes, with various disabilities or illnesses who were abandoned or abused. Some find forever homes; some stay with me for years until they pass away. I'm not always successful at saving each of them, but that doesn't stop me from trying my best.

It was far more joyful a life than firing all those people who had been like family to me—people who trusted me and deserved better.

It's been a journey filled with joy, tears, heartache and, ultimately, an immense sense of satisfaction in knowing I was doing something both morally and socially responsible. Despite the occasional heart-breaking moment of releasing an animal I had grown attached to, I was grateful that I had walked away from corporate life.

The sudden influx of Fiona's wealth, though?

It might have just shoved me back into it.

I left the serenity of the isolation room and walked into the kitchen.

Ellie was frantically typing on her laptop, Darla leaning over her shoulder.

The two leaned against the old wooden kitchen table with its uneven surface, chipped corners, and decades of gouges no one had ever bothered to fix. I surveyed the room and saw everything in hyper-focus now that someone was handing me millions of dollars.

"Are you girls okay?" I asked, coming to a stop in front of them. "I assume you heard what happened at the lawyer's—"

"Oh, I heard," Evie said, not looking up from her screen. "It's all over JuxtaPorte. Twenty-seven million dollars buys an awful lot of games, Mom. I'm adding every single one I've ever wanted to my cart, so as soon as we get that inheritance—"

"The shelter gets the money, Evie, not us."

Evie's head snapped up. "Wait, what?"

"We, personally, are not inheriting anything," I told her quickly, nipping her PC gaming greed-filled shopping spree in the bud. "We can't spend it on whatever we want to for ourselves, hon. The money's for the cats, and it goes to the nonprofit."

"Seriously? We get nothing?"

"Seriously."

Darla and Evie stared at me, eyes wide with disbelief and shock. Clearly, the town gossip posts left out a big fact about "my" inheritance.

The part where it technically wasn't mine.

"Well, okay, let's think about this. What about

Straggle?" Darla suggested, pointing to something on the screen. "That's a cat game. Cats all over the place are going nuts about it. Posts are all over the internet—we could take pictures of the cat watching the game and then it's a business expense when we post them on SocialBook. That works, right?"

"Mom?" Evie looked at me hopefully.

I sighed. "Fine. One cat game. But that's it. No more after that. And we are not turning this place into the Four Seasons of cat shelters either, got it?"

"I...um...sure," Evie answered, confused. "No problem."

"What about the news people?" Darla asked. "Are they still outside?"

"Yep." I glanced outside and saw Landon forcefully directing the reporters off my lawn and onto the sidewalk in front of the shelter. "They're camped out front like a bunch of vultures."

"I don't understand why they're so interested in a shelter inheriting money," Evie said, leaning forward in her chair as her eyes went from side to side, scanning the information on the computer screen. She stopped and sat up quickly, her face brightening. "Ooh! A special edition!" Suddenly her gaze shifted upward to meet mine; her cheeks flushed as if she anticipated my disapproval. "What?"

I pinched the bridge of my nose.

Deep breaths, Ellie.

"Nothing," I said after mentally counting to ten.

"Just don't get too excited about this, okay? We don't know what's going to happen yet. Let's just take it one day at a time. No need to go overboard."

She pursed her lips and bit her lower one, considering. "It's just one game—they could really use some entertainment," Evie said, half to herself. "Maybe they'd like watching a game? On the computer?" She paused, glancing around the room as if asking the opinion of the cats lounging around.

Darla jumped in. "Really, Ms. Rockwell, the special edition comes with cat toys and—"

"Just one game, ladies," I told them. "It's about what the money can do for these animals. It gives us a chance to save so many lives. To make a real difference in the world. And that is why we need to be very careful about how we spend it and what we spend it on. People only get chances like this once in a lifetime."

"You're right, Mom. We should probably set up a meeting with a financial adviser or something to make sure we do this right. Right?" Evie said.

Oh. Yeah, that was a good idea, actually.

"Of course!" Darla agreed.

"Absolutely," I said, relief flooding through me. She seemed to take this seriously. "And in the meantime, we need to keep things as normal around here as possible. For us, and the cats. That means no talking to reporters, no grandiose purchases—"

"Totally," Evie said, her attention still on the screen in front of her.

Darla and Evie had their heads together, their eyes sparkling with excitement as they talked in low voices about which video games they should get eventually, once I loosened up a bit.

I shook my head as I flopped down into a wing chair in the living room, my head spinning and my body suddenly feeling heavy. I felt myself getting more and more anxious. What if something went wrong? The responsibility of making sure we did right by the cats, that we honored Fiona's gift, that we took care of Belladonna without—

Digby jumped on my lap and licked my chin.

"Do I look that frazzled, Digs?" I asked.

The nine-year-old cat meowed something that sounded like an affirmative response.

Chapter Fifteen

"Step back," Laurie said, her voice firm yet gentle.

Landon, behind her, nodded.

And behind him?

Laurie's veterinary assistant.

I stared at her. "What are you all doing here?"

"Josephine called me." She smoothed her long brown hair and adjusted her oversized sweatshirt. "Landon, too. Are you going to make a move? I don't want to be on a news camera looking like a wreck."

I moved.

Landon explained that Josephine Reynolds, a Silver Circle board member and local attorney, had called earlier that day, informing them they needed to be at the shelter at 7 o'clock on the dot.

"So, we're here," Laurie added and moved, uninvited, toward the main living room where Matt, Darla, and Evie already were. "She should be here any minute to explain. We got this."

I looked between Laurie and Landon, both of whom were now standing in the living room. I could see the eagerness in their eyes, but I just felt lost. "Explain what?" I asked hesitantly.

"Don't worry," Laurie responded, patting my shoulder.

"Are you going to keep this property, or turn Wardwell Manor into a shelter?" Matt asked Evie.

"The Manor is already ten times the size of this house, and while it'd be a shame that all the work we did here would go to waste, the cats' needs would outweigh my selfish desires to stay here." Evie answered with a wistful smile. "I love this house. I have a lot of wonderful memories here."

"We haven't decided," I told him as I squeezed by to grab a glass of iced tea. "How could we decide when we haven't even discussed everything? I need time to catch my breath, Matt."

"You're right, of course," Matt said. "But you know that no matter what you decide, we'll be here to help."

"Yes, of course," I answered absently, my attention focused on a Siamese cat perched on the windowsill.

"It's going to be a great opportunity for the shelter," Laurie called from the kitchen as she prepared chips and dip for everyone. "You'll have the space and resources to do so much more. Just think of all the people you could help, Ellie. You could move beyond just rescues to behavior assistance for overwhelmed owners, educating the community. Sliding scale animal boarding. Oh!" She stuck her head out. "You could train therapy animals."

"Are there therapy cats?" Matt asked.

"There have to be," Evie told him. "Not everyone likes dogs."

"You're wrong. Everyone likes dogs," Laurie disagreed. "You could expand into rescuing—"

"No," I told her. "I came out here to start a cat rescue. Not a generic animal shelter. The quickest way to screw up is to be everything to everyone."

"Spoilsport," Laurie said. "What about little hand-bag-sized dogs?"

"Have you got any communication from your ex-husband?" Laurie's veterinary assistant, Francis Higgins, inquired.

Francis was a brand new veterinary assistant fresh out of college. She wore thick glasses that magnified her baby browns and had brown hair that hung down to her shoulders. She was also known for being brusque to the point of being unintentionally rude.

I stole a quick glance at Evie, whose eyes were wide as she nervously shifted her gaze between Francis and me. "No."

She continued talking, apparently unaware of the unease that had crept across my face. "I bet he already knows about your windfall. It's all over the internet."

I could feel my stomach tighten as I thought of him

discovering the inheritance. "It's not my windfall, so it has nothing to do with him," I told the young woman.

Laurie's face twisted into a comical expression as she said, "She's right, though. That man would sell out his mother to a bookie if he got a commission on it," Laurie said. Mid-chuckle, Laurie's expression dropped as she reached over to place her hand on Evie's arm. "Oh, Evie, I'm sorry. I forgot he's your—"

"Birth father," she told Laurie, her mouth twisted into a sour line. "I haven't spoken to the man since I was six years old. Insult him all you want. I promise you, I've called him worse in therapy. He deserves worse."

It was true.

Well, not that he deserved worse.

It was hard for me to hate a man I'd married and had a child with, though Mason's behavior made it a greater potential than it should be.

I'd heard from my ex-husband, Mason Miller, more recently than Evie had. He'd contact me every so often—making threats and demanding money—but for some reason, he'd forget how to use a phone on his own daughter's birthday.

It also never seemed to occur to him that the money he demanded would come right out of the household budget raising and supporting his medically fragile daughter—money he did not contribute to, since he hadn't paid child support but two times in his life.

Anyway, Evie was so disgusted with him she'd asked to change her last name as soon as she turned eighteen.

I gladly paid for it.

"Your father can't get his hands on one red cent, Evette." Our heads turned to find the nonprofit's attorney, Josephine Reynolds, with all her glittery pink eye shadow and gold nail polish, standing in the doorway.

She hadn't bothered to knock.

"Fiona left the money to the nonprofit, not your mother. If Mason Miller so much as tries to make inroads, I'll smash his walnuts in a vise of paperwork so strong the pieces left won't even be suited for a pie." The fake gold earrings that hung from the holes in the lobes of her ears matched her nail polish. "No charge."

"Birth father," Evie corrected. "Hey, Josie."

Josie looked like an experimental stylist helped her dress for a Hollywood premiere attended by seventies David Bowie fans, but she was actually the rescue's attorney. The lawyer no-nonsense woman who didn't take crap from anyone—and she was fiercely protective of me, Evie, and Silver Circle Rescue (for reasons I could never quite fathom.)

Josie smiled and waved at Evie as she continued her story. "So, Mason can't get his hands on the money," Josie explained. "And since everyone's here, we should probably get started."

"Get started with what?" Laurie asked. "You made it sound like we were just coming to support Ellie emotionally."

"Oh, really? You made it sound like it was something more," I pointed out.

She shifted her weight and looked away, her hands tugging at the ends of her long sleeve shirt. "Well, yeah. Caught me. But in my defense, if I just said we were all here for emotional support, you wouldn't have opened the door," Laurie said.

"And we are here for emotional support," Josie agreed. "But there's other things at issue here, and it's time for the board meeting."

Matt shifted nervously in his seat. "Oops, I didn't know there was a board meeting," he said, and he rose from his chair.

Josie's eyes widened. "Where are you going, young man?" she asked sharply. "Did I tell you to leave?"

Matt froze. "But I'm not on the board. Should I even be here?"

"You should," Josie answered him.

Matt's face betrayed surprise, and he shifted his weight back down. "Okay. But why?"

"Right now," she began, "Ellie, Evie and I are on the board. It's all well and good for a small nonprofit like ours—twenty-five thousand dollars in the bank, a piece of property, and a heap of debt—but for a multi-million dollar one with court reporting requirements, that won't cut it." She pushed a stack of papers across the table. "This is what I propose."

I stared at the papers and swallowed hard.

What I didn't have a handle on Josie, apparently, did.

Josephine adjusted her glasses and clasped her hands on the conference table, her gaze bouncing between Laurie and me. "I propose that to avoid any conflict of interest, I leave the board and represent Silver Circle formally as its attorney—you can certainly afford me now."

"You could also donate your services," Landon said with his eyebrows raised.

She ignored him. "I suggest you remain President, Ellie. Laurie can take the Vice President position." She paused, her face turning slightly pensive. "The only issue is, most non-profit organizations don't pay their board members or appoint paid staff to serve on the board."

"Wait a minute. Am I losing my salary?" I asked in a panicked tone.

"I didn't say you couldn't be paid. I said most nonprofits do not pay their board members. There are risks and benefits here to going against the grain," Josephine told me, and then looked around at everyone else. "You, Evie, Darla, and Matt are the core of the staff at Silver Circle. If you all serve as staff and board members, some things may require a...deeper explanation. The state may be further up your business, the Judge a bit more concerned."

"I don't care if anyone's up in our business," I responded with a shrug.

Matt's eyes widened in disbelief as he asked, "Wait, are we getting paid now?"

Darla's mouth dropped open, her face illuminated with the hint of a smile. She could barely contain her excitement as she breathed, "Wow, that's..."

"Yes. These would be jobs and board positions. Well, for you two." She looked at Matt and Darla and flicked her wrist dismissively. "We'd like you to serve as board members besides the formal positions." Josephine looked around. "You, Francis, will just be a board member."

"Oh." Francis nodded shyly. "Um, okay. If you need me to."

My eyebrows shot up in surprise. Josie and I had not discussed this.

"We would?" I asked her, my voice uncertain.

"Yes, Ellie. We would," she answered with a confident voice. Her stern expression softened, and her gaze shifted around the room. "You all have been the most dedicated to the shelter's cause, even before its fortune changed. We need board members and staff who share that same passion and commitment, so there's less of a risk of mismanagement."

"I don't know," Matt said. His forehead creased in worry as he spoke. "I don't know the first thing about being on a board."

"Me neither," Darla said. "I can't even keep track of my apartment's bills. I actually lost my parking space because I forgot the payment was separate."

"That's why you have an accountant, Darla. We'll hire an accountant. I'll represent you—the nonprofit, not you people individually—as an attorney."

We stared at her.

"Oh, for goodness' sake, it will be fine—and it needs to be now." Josie spoke with an authoritative voice. "If you two want to be part of the board, we need you to step up. If you don't, we're going to have to go out into the community to look for additional members, and I don't want to do that."

"Why?" I asked.

"You know who likes to serve on boards? Jessa Winthrop." Josie let the name linger in the air, watching as a wave of uneasiness rolled across the room. "That woman drives around town, peering in through the windows of nonprofits to see if there are board seats available."

Darla and Matt looked at each other and sighed, but there was no further hedging.

Josie looked at Evie, who shrugged and nodded.

"You'll all be fine. I'll teach you," Josie said with a shrug and a grin, as if she had all the power and personality necessary to be great at everything. "It's easy as hell. You don't have to have a brain in your head to be on a non-profit board." Josephine told everyone. "We can hire someone to go through our accounting procedures, budgets, financial policy..."

As Josephine prattled on, I felt queasy.

"...but you approve the budget and sign the financial

report. Very simple." Josephine shrugged. "But you shouldn't do that alone, anyway, Ellie. I think it will help you if you bring your plans to everyone else, anyway. Get different perspectives."

The queasy feeling grew.

"Are you all right, Ellie?" Josie inquired, concerned.

"Yeah, it's nothing." I shook my head. "It's just a lot to take in."

"That's what I'm here for." Josephine cleared her throat. "I feel like a lot of this blindsided surprise could have been avoided, by the way, if I'd been at the lawyer's office with you from the get go."

"Yeah, maybe. I didn't expect what happened. I didn't think I'd need a lawyer."

"Who would have expected something like that?" Darla asked.

"I know," Josie said. "But I'm sorry you had to deal with that alone, Ellie. I should have been there."

I looked up to find Belladonna high on a cat perch, staring directly at me.

Her golden-yellow eyes glowed with a feral intensity.

"Let's get moving, then," Josie said, but she sounded far away.

I was captivated by the way Bella's eyes seemed to penetrate me. I wondered what secrets this mysterious cat held—what had she witnessed in her time with Fiona? Did she know why Fiona had donated all of her money to the shelter?

"What do you know?" I whispered.

The cat's fur seemed to glow like liquid silver in the light of the full moon that shone through the windows, and I couldn't help but admire its enigmatic beauty. Cats always seemed so wise; it was almost as though she could understand everything we said. Like she could read my thoughts about—

"Sorry, Ellie?" Landon asked. "What did you say?"

"You're not okay," Josie said. "You look pale as a ghost."

I slowly shook my head from side to side. "I'm fine."

"Do you want to meditate? I have my yoga mats in the car." Josie squinted her eyes, her forehead creasing as she analyzed me with a look of deep concentration. "Do I need to call my acupuncturist and get her here? Maybe your chi is blocked."

I shook my head slowly once more, trying to find a small smile I could offer that would get Josie off my back with her crazy new age pin cushion solutions to everything. "Its fine, Josie. I'm fine. Today's just been a little overwhelming."

Overwhelming.

I kept saying that word.

Josie accepted my words with a slight nod. "I'll try to keep that in mind, but I have to admit I just can't ever get too far away from my micromanaging. It's a disease. I'll try to loosen up."

"Thanks," I responded wryly.

Loosen up.

That was funny.

Josephine Reynolds couldn't loosen up if she tried.

She was efficient as she passed around the papers to the people in the room while her long, glossy fingernails glinted golden in the light. "Let's get a move on, people. Sign that, and you are a board member. I want those dated today." Josie flung ball-point pens across the room. "Let's hop to it."

"Hey," Francis said. "Since when does a board just get dictated to like this?" She looked around the room, her gaze shifting from each person to the next as if searching for support. "I mean, why didn't you vote on this? Shouldn't the old board members do that?"

"Does anyone have any objections?" Josie glared at Evie and me, her eyes demanding agreement.

We both nodded obediently.

Josie shifted her gaze to Francis, who shrunk back against the couch. "Happy now?"

"I guess so," Francis said meekly.

"Good." Josie pointed at the papers in Francis's hand. "Sign them."

Francis hastily scribbled her name before handing the documents back to Josie.

Chapter Sixteen

I wished Josephine had been with me when I met the lawyer. She had a knack for getting her way in any situation, and I was sure she would have had the perfect thing to say at that moment.

But even if she had been there, who knows if she could have prepared me for the shocking news? I guess I'll never know.

Because I ignored that I was close friends with a lawyer.

And I trucked over there all by myself.

Because I needed no help from anyone.

As usual.

It might be my biggest weakness—that I always try to do everything myself and then feel overwhelmed.

Because no one's helping me.

I fully admit it makes no sense.

"Ellie!" Josie said sharply.

"Huh?"

"Sign."

I signed.

After we all signed the papers, Josie called an impromptu board meeting.

"A board meeting?" Landon asked. His face was a combination of annoyance and confusion. "What were we doing before?"

With a silent glare at Landon, Josie launched into a presentation of her proposed temporary operational budget, explaining in swift detail what our responsibilities would be. She was thorough and patient with us as we asked questions and tried to understand the nuances of the change we'd all signed up for.

We voted to hire me, Evie, Darla, and Matt as full-time staff members, each with a salary commiserate with their experience and the size of our team—around thirty-eight thousand dollars, give or take.

Laurie urged me to take more salary than the others, but I refused. "It's what I make now, more or less, and it's fine. We live at the shelter, so a lot of my bills are split between us and the nonprofit."

"You going to continue with that?" Josie asked with a slight, barely detectable edge.

"Of course. Why wouldn't we?"

"It's just a lot of extra paperwork, is all. I figured maybe you wanted to do something a bit more professional." Josie paused. "Like live in a house without a hundred or more cats."

Digby, who was walking by, cast one eye at Josie and hissed a warning.

"You tell her, Digs," Evie called after the cat.

"One thing at a time, Josephine Overkill," Laurie said.

"I hate that nickname."

"Then dial it back so it doesn't fit you so well. Look, all I'm saying, Ellie," Laurie said as she handed me a glass of wine, "is that a little less than forty thousand a year? It's not enough to live on. Especially not in this town with high-dollar Austin creeping out here every day. And while those three folks are super important, you do the lion's share of the work."

"I don't care about the money."

Josie sighed and adjusted her glasses. "Yes, we all know what a selfless martyr you are, but we need to think about the future of this organization. If we're going to make it successful, then everyone needs to be compensated fairly. And that includes you."

"Money's not everything. I made over six figures when I worked in Austin, and it didn't make me happy. In fact, I was absolutely miserable." Working my way up for years, two positions down from the CEO of a publicly traded company—only to find it wasn't what I expected and nothing I wanted. "Just—money isn't everything."

"You hated the company, Ellie, not the money," Landon said, piling on.

The room fell silent for a moment as all eyes turned toward me.

I said what I had to say. They could stare at me all night for all I care.

After a few more moments of uncomfortable silence, Josie cleared her throat and spoke up again.

"Listen, I'm going to say it one more time. You're doing amazing work here, and you deserve to be compensated for it. Just let us—as the board—all pay you what's fair and average and the least you could expect in the position you have."

"No. I said no and I—"

"Because if you don't, we're just going to outvote you and do it anyway, Ellie." Josie leaned forward. "We're on the board. We can do that."

I slowly lowered my chin in agreement, my eyes downcast in defeat.

Josie called the vote, and with that last vote, the meeting was over—and I was the head of a multi-million dollar cat rescue in Tablerock, Texas.

Everyone stayed.

I looked around the room and realized we'd divided ourselves into groups. Evie, Matt, Darla, and Francis, all in their early to midtwenties, gathered at the back of the room near the catio. Josephine, Laurie, and I, all in our late forties to early fifties, gathered on the other side of the room.

The young crowd was loose, comfortable and all smiles. Excited about their new jobs, new salaries. My older crowd, on the other hand, was much more reserved —and chose wine instead of beer.

Landon stood between the two groups like a bridge, his face a mix of both optimism and anxiety as he stood beneath a cat tree, puzzledly looking up at Belladonna. His hands were motionless against his sides, as if he were afraid to make the slightest movement, while Belladonna continued to purr loudly, her tail swishing and her eyes half-closed in pleasure at his rapt attention.

"She sure is a beautiful cat," he said.

Belladonna stretched toward Landon and lightly pressed her head against his, as if accepting his presence and returning the compliment.

Manipulative sociopath, I thought.

"Ellie!"

"Sorry, what?" I asked Laurie, trying to pay attention.

"I said you're going to have to get comfortable talking about money," Laurie said.

"I don't want to talk about money," I said. "I just don't."

"That's not an option you get to choose anymore," Josie said with a shrug. "You can want to or not want to talk about it, but you have to deal with it all the same."

I knew she was right, but I didn't have to be happy about it.

I was startled when a sudden, sharp sound cut through the air. I quickly realized it was the sound of a knock on the door, so I got out of my seat and went to answer it.

"Deputy Markham," I said, a confused expression on my face. "It's kind of late." I scanned for a cat carrier, but he wasn't carrying anything. "What can I do for you?"

He nodded his head and stepped inside without being invited in and without taking off his hat—a cowboy-style black straw Resistol.

Once inside, Markham glanced around. "I'm sorry to disturb you so late in the evening, but I have some news that I think you should know."

Well, it wasn't that late. "Oh?"

"A member of the Tablerock Police found a gun near your entrance gate earlier this evening. We don't know who it belongs to yet, but I wanted to make sure you were informed."

"If the gun was found by the city police, why are you here?"

Deputy Markham cleared his throat and adjusted his hat before speaking as if to buy himself time. "We don't know who owns this gun or if it is connected to either of the murders just yet, but the mayor thought it would be best to hand it over to the county so we can investigate further."

Did that mean Beau was shot, then? Or did they

think the two murders were linked? I mentally rolled my eyes—of course, the two murders were linked. How could they not be? And what, pray tell, did the mayor have to do with a police investigation?

I faked a nonchalant response. "I see."

Markham nodded. "It could be a crucial piece of evidence for solving these cases."

Laurie and Landon stepped closer, wearing worried expressions. Meanwhile, Josie moved to my side and shifted into a battle stance, her body tense like a coiled spring. Hell, I could practically feel her taking aim, steadying herself for the perfect moment to start a barrage of questions.

"You said a member of the police found the gun on this property?"

Markham nodded. "Yes, ma'am."

"Did they have a warrant?" Josie had her hands on her hips, her head cocked slightly to one side as she waited for Markham to respond.

The deputy cleared his throat and his friendly demeanor cooled. "Aren't you a civil attorney and not a criminal one, Mrs. Reynolds?"

The lawyer's eyes glinted like a pair of razors, her lips thinning with irritation. "That's not an adequate response, Deputy."

Markham's answer was automatic, in a voice as stony as his features. "No, they did not possess a warrant. Ma'am."

"Deputy," Josie snapped her gaze up to meet the

deputy's, her voice as hard as steel," I may be just a small civil attorney from the country, but I do believe ya'll need a warrant to take people's property like this." Her drawl was thick and pointed as her words cut through the air and echoed off the walls.

"You know she's right, Don," Landon said with a gentle head tilt.

"Is it your gun, Eleanor?" the deputy asked me while ignoring the opinionated peanut gallery. "Do you know anything about it?"

Before I could utter a word, Josie shot back. "Why are you just asking those questions now?"

Belladonna hissed from her perch on the wall.

Deputy Markham scanned us all, his lips forming a tight line. A nerve twitched in his jaw, and he let out a long breath. "Look, this isn't how I wanted this to go."

"No? Which part was she supposed to roll over for?" Josie asked.

The deputy squirmed, trying to appear congenial. His tone carried a hint of menace. "No. No, ma'am. But an officer saw the firearm and retrieved it on the grounds of public safety. What I cannot fathom is why everyone is getting so... bothered." He let the word hang in the air, his gaze slowly sweeping the room in warning.

"Bothered about pesky things like civil rights? Constitutional protections? Due process?" Josie's face was hardened into a mask of determination. "So you think it's all right to trample civil rights and constitutional protections as long as you can get away with it?

Who do you think you are, coming onto the shelter's property without a warrant?" The challenge in her voice was unmistakable.

The deputy's hands were locked tight, knuckles white. His jaw clenched like a vise as he spoke. "Just as the mayor said, it'd be better if this were handed over to the county..." But before he could finish, Josie shut him down again.

"The mayor can think whatever she likes, Don," she said as she crossed her arms, "but the fact is, the county and city police just arrogantly trampled on this shelter's constitutional rights." She paused and crossed her arms over her chest. "Now, are you going to apologize?"

Deputy Markham sighed, his face revealing the strain of the situation.

"Mom, what's going on?" Ellie asked.

The kids moved across the room with looks of concern.

Josie took a sharp step back, putting her hand on my daughter's shoulder. She glared at Markham, a chill in her gaze. "It's just a reminder that no one escapes justice. Everyone has to follow the law." Softening only slightly, she added, "It's important to remember that no matter how high someone is, they still have to respect the rights of those around them."

Markham shifted his hat on his head and cleared his throat again to speak. When he did, it was with an air of resignation. "Yes ma'am. I apologize. It won't happen again."

Josie nodded in acceptance, her eyes still narrowed in suspicion. "Good."

"Okay, that's settled. What do we do about this gun?" Landon asked.

"Gun?" Matt asked, startled. "What gun?"

"Oh, don't worry about it," Josie said with a wave. "If it happened the way he said, that cop probably didn't need a warrant. You only need one if there is a reasonable expectation of privacy and no probable cause. A gun visible from the road sounds like plain sight to me."

My jaw dropped. "Then why did you just go after him like that?"

"I'm a lawyer." Josie smiled and shrugged. "The police should always be able to defend their actions," she explained. "That, and it's always good to sharpen and hone my skills when given the opportunity."

Markham's body was rigid, a stance of silent strength despite the fatigue that seemed to radiate from him. "Yes, ma'am."

"By the way, Don—who was the cop that found the gun?"

Markham sighed. After a long pause, he finally answered, "Officer Winthrop found it during rush hour today. Around 4 p.m. or so down by the mailbox."

Like a shot, Landon stepped forward.

"It's probably best if we let the police handle this one," he said in an authoritative tone of voice. "Don, thanks for coming by." He held out his hand, and the deputy shook it firmly, both men keeping their eyes trained on each other.

Don Markham nodded goodbye to the women, tipping his hat like an old-fashioned gentleman—I guess we didn't rate a handshake—before walking back out to his car.

"Someone's lying," Landon said once the door closed behind the deputy.

Josie looked at him, and then to the others in the room. "What do you mean?" she asked.

"I followed Ellie back to her place from the park, and I didn't see any police trying to corral those yokels out front," Landon said, running a hand through his hair. "In fact, I was pretty pissed off watching it. It looked like a swarm of angry bees running all over the front."

"What does that have to do with the gun?" I asked.

"It has to do with the gun because there was no cop out there on the street to see a gun by the mailbox," Landon said, shaking his head. "Not at 3 p.m., not at 4 p.m., and not at 5 p.m."

Laurie had a look of disbelief on her face as she stared at Landon. "Jeez, Landon, how long were you out there?" the vet asked.

"As long as I needed to be," Landon said, a determined look on his face. "But in general? From about 3 to 6."

"We all met here at 7." I stared at him. "Did you eat?"

"I grabbed some tacos at Pepper Jalisco's, but that's not important here. The important thing here is I didn't see a single Tablerock Police Department squad car in front of the house. Not driving by, not parked, nothing." Landon's jaw was set in a determined expression, and his eyes were steady. "I didn't see anyone stop, and I didn't see any officers get out, pick something up, and get back in. No one picked up a gun at 4 p.m. What he claimed happened did not happen. I would've seen it."

"I know there's been two murders, but aren't we getting a little paranoid?" Matt asked the group.

Josie shook her head. "No, Matt," she said. "We're being cautious. If the police are lying about finding the gun, we need to know why."

"Okay, I hear you," I said. "But I work with Don all the time, Josie. I don't think he'd lie."

"Maybe he was lied to, Ellie. Don't you think we'd have seen something about it in the news if it happened?" Laurie pointed toward the front of the house. "Those vultures have been scanning for some angle to this story all day. You don't think police traipsing through the weeds and coming out with a tossed gun would have been rated newsworthy?"

"There's nothing on SocialBook at all about a gun being found at our place," Evie said, lit up by the soft blue light of her cell phone. "Let me check one more group." After a few moments, she looked up with a puzzled expression and said, "Yeah, no. There's nothing here. Nothing at all."

Laurie looked at Landon. "Maybe the police haven't released anything about it yet?"

"Who did they say found the gun?" Evie asked. "Officer Winthrop?"

At the mention of the officer's name, Evie's head snapped up. "Officer Winthrop? Are you sure?"

"Yes, honey," I said. "Why?"

"Wait a minute," she said.

Evie quickly typed Officer Winthrop's name into her phone and, a moment later, she muttered, "I knew it. Officer Winthrop is the mayor's son! Joel Winthrop."

"Well, I'm a little embarrassed at not catching that," Josie said.

Darla shuddered. "I went to school with that snot-nosed maggot. His mother was always bailing him out of trouble no matter how deep the muck. He swaggers around, acting like he owns the place, filled with delusions of grandeur due to his privilege."

"I went to school with him, too," Matt said. "Darla's not wrong. That guy was a major jerk. He strutted around with a giant sense of entitlement, like he was better than everyone else."

The kids were all in their midtwenties, which would make Joel Winthrop right around the same age, right? I mentally calculated again. Yeah, the ages of all these people don't quite make sense. "Does anyone know how old Mayor Winthrop is?" I asked.

"I don't know," Landon said with a shrug. "I'm better off not asking women their ages. I don't think that's allowed anymore."

Evie tapped her fingers against her phone. "She'll turn fifty-seven in a couple months."

"Is there anything not on the internet?" Laurie asked.

"Yep." Evie waved her phone. "That a gun was found at our house."

Josie's eyes met mine. "Why do you ask, Ellie?"

"Well, it just occurred to me that Fiona Blackwell was in her eighties, right? Late seventies, early eighties?" There was a weird sense of anticipation in the air, like the pause when lightning cracks and thunder is still to come. No cats meowed, even. "So her husband must have been around the same age, right? I mean, I ran into him a few times around town. He was pretty old."

"You might wanna watch it with the 'old' designations," Laurie said. "We're not exactly spring chickens."

"Speak for yourself," said Josie. "I cluck just fine."

"I think they were around the same age," Darla, who'd worked for them previously, agreed. "I don't know exactly how old he was, but he was Fiona's age. Not ya'll's."

"That's a huge age difference in a relationship," I pointed out.

Josie shrugged. "Lot's of people have May-December romances."

"Jessa would have been thirty-seven or so when they

started their affair, right? I'm not trying to be rude, but dating a wealthy guy in his sixties must be a very different experience from having an affair with an eighty-year-old." I looked at Josie. "Jessa Winthrop was at the lawyer's office today, and she certainly seemed to expect something out of that will. More than what she got."

"And she came over here claiming Belladonna was hers," Evie added. "Like, was really insistent."

Belladonna hissed.

"Did she, now?" Josie's expression was thoughtful. "We need to get a hold of Beau Blackwell's will."

"Why?" Laurie asked, confused.

Josie intently leaned forward, her eyes blazing with suspicion. "Because if Jessa Winthrop was expecting a windfall, then Joel Winthrop was probably expecting to get something out of these inheritances, too—and since he didn't, he might have had a reason to claim he found a gun here."

"What?" I blurted, taken aback.

"To pin the murder on you," Josie replied with a steely edge in her voice.

"What?" I gasped, my mind spinning with disbelief. "You can't be serious."

Belladonna meowed a purr-like chime that seemed to hang in the air.

Chapter Seventeen

BELLADONNA GAVE ME A SIDE GLANCE, HER GAZE AS golden as the morning sun. "Your friend with the grating voice could be on to something, you know," she purred, her fur standing on end. "Someone might set you up to take the blame for Fiona's untimely demise." Her claws extended. "A shame, too. I had just started teaching you the finer points of caring for me and I'd hate to see all my efforts go to waste." Belladonna let out a soft sigh, as if to emphasize her point.

Evie and I exchanged concerned glances.

We'd crept down the creaking hallway in the early morning darkness to speak privately with the cat, and found Belladonna perched atop the cat tree in the isolation room, a silent sentry watching the door.

"Anything else?" Evie asked.

She advised us to avoid dark alleys and public places after sunset. "Never travel alone; always bring a companion and be armed to the teeth with swords, knives, and daggers. You soft, vulnerable humans are completely defenseless without weapons."

"I'm not getting an escort." Evie looked at the cat, an odd expression on her face. "And we can't leave the house like we're going noodling."

I frowned. "What's noodling?"

"Hunting with your bare hands. Catfish specifically, but I saw someone use the term for hunting snakes, too."

I looked at her oddly. "How do you even know that?"

"The internet."

Belladonna yawned. "Like I said. If you die, my time is wasted."

"Why did Jessa Winthrop claim you were her cat?" I asked.

"Because Jessa Winthrop, the mayor, is a liar. She has always viewed Fiona with envy. It was not enough for her to have that hairless rat as a mate. She desired the home, money, and social standing. She likely believed that by claiming me, she would gain leverage over my mistress's estate. Ultimately, it is for my care, after all." Belladonna's voice was low and cold. "However, it backfired. I cannot tolerate liars, and my loyalty to Fiona extends beyond the very end."

"Let me ask you something," I said, after mulling over her words. "Do you think Jessa could be behind Fiona's death?"

The cat gazed around, her shining yellow eyes bright in the dimness. "It's possible," she meowed cautiously. "I

207

know the mayor was angry when Fiona demanded the bastard be sent away—"

"Whoa, language, Bella," Evie told her.

Her head swiveled. "But that is what he is. A bastard. A child born from a tryst out of wedlock."

"Rude and we don't say that anymore, but you're a cat, so we'll let it slide. What child are you talking about?" I asked, wincing at the word.

"The child Beau and Jessa Winthrop had." Belladonna yawned again.

Evie and I looked like a pair of surprised fish, our eyes wide and our mouths hanging open. If we'd seen a monster truck painted like the Pink Panther rushing toward the house from the field out back, we wouldn't have looked more surprised.

"Jessa was no doubt hoping to gain control of the estate along with Beau after my mistress passed away, so in that sense, yes, I think she could be—"

"Wait," I said, holding up a hand. "Beau and Jessa had a kid?" Evie's eyes narrowed. "Are you talking about Joel Winthrop?"

I shook my head. "No way. Joel is in his midtwenties, and they'd only been together twenty years when he passed." I looked at Evie. "Can you check your phone?"

"You know, you could check on your phone, Mom."

I glared.

Evie whipped out her phone and tapped furiously. Seconds later, she thrust the device into my hands, the light from the screen painting her face with a blue pallor.

"Here it is, you're right. Joel Winthrop is twenty-six. On SocialBook, his father is listed as Jake Winthrop." She scrolled and pointed. "Girlfriend works for the county." She scrolled again. "His father died twenty-five years ago." She looked at Belladonna. "So then who are you—"

Belladonna silenced Evie with a dismissive wave of her paw. "Joel is likely the result of this marriage, or he may be the result of an affair between Jessa and another person. However, this is not the child I am referring to. I never said it was."

I raised my eyebrows. "There's another one?"

Belladonna nodded. "There is, indeed. Fiona and Beau never spoke publicly about the child, and Jessa attempted to keep the child hidden from the world."

I couldn't believe what I was hearing, and a million questions flooded my mind. How did this happen? Who was the child? Was it Beau's or someone else's? Where did he go after the birth? Why hadn't anyone heard of this before?

Evie seemed equally stunned and opened her mouth to ask more questions.

Belladonna leveled a stern gaze at us. "If you're going to ask me questions, I don't know any more than that," the cat said firmly, as if sensing our shock and curiosity over the matter. "Well, I know the child's name was Jackson—"

"Winthrop or Blackwell?" Evie asked.

"My mistress was horrified by the unborn child. She warned Beau that she would divorce him and leave him with nothing if the child was brought out in public. She didn't want him anywhere she would be obligated to see him." Belladonna's tail swished behind her like an agitated pendulum. "I advised her to kill the creature as soon as it was born, but she stated that humans have rules against such behavior." She sniffed. "Although you wouldn't think so after all this mess."

I leaned forward, my curiosity piqued. "So what happened to Jackson?"

"Beau was greedy. He wanted to keep his comfortable life, so he refused to acknowledge the child or accept responsibility for it. Jessa sent Jackson away to Dallas to be raised by her sister. It shielded them all from the consequences of their actions."

"When did this happen?"

"About eighteen years ago, soon after they started the affair."

Evie nodded. "What happened to Jackson after she gave him up?"

Belladonna stretched out in an early morning sunbeam and closed her eyes, seemingly done with the conversation. "No one knows. He was gone from the town before his first birthday, and his name has never been spoken since."

"A hidden child," I said.

"A hidden, secret, illegitimate child born during an

affair," Evie corrected. "It's like we stepped into a soap opera. How did this stay under wraps for so many years?"

It was unbelievable that Jackson had been so callously forgotten, a casualty of an age where secrets stayed behind closed doors and no one had ever heard of social media. I thought of poor little Jackson, sent away in shame and secrecy.

It made me sad to think of him growing up with such rejection.

"We should tell someone," Evie said.

I cursed fluently enough to widen Evie's eyes. "Tell who, exactly? And where in the nine hells do you expect us to say we found out this information? No one knows about the blasted platter but us."

Evie slowly averted her gaze. Her forehead scrunched up in a worrisome way, and she nervously nibbled on her bottom lip. When her eyes finally flicked back to me, her words came out as a meek mumble. "Now, don't get mad. Umm...I...well, so...okay, I may have mentioned something about the enchanted dish and conversational cats to Matt last night."

My jaw plummeted in disbelief as my mind scrambled to grasp her words. "Evie!" I gasped, aghast. "What were you thinking?"

"I know!"

"Obviously not!"

"Well, it's a hard secret to keep, okay? It's just the biggest thing that ever happened to me—well, besides my three open heart surgeries. And the pacemaker. And the Make a Wish trip to Disney World—"

"Okay, stop." My shoulders slumped in frustration and I dropped my face into my palms. "I blabbed to Laurie about the magic platter and its talking cats at dinner the other night," I told her, my words muffled.

"What was that?" She asked me, her tone sharp. "I didn't quite hear you."

I lifted my head and met her gaze. I'd already made the mistake, so may as well own up to it. "I told Laurie," I blurted, my voice shaking a bit.

She groaned loudly, her hands clutched her head in frustration. "At least I didn't tell him in public! Jeez, Mom!"

"I know," I admitted. "We're terrible at this."

"Why did you do that?" She shook her head, her face showing a mix of disbelief and amusement.

As I was about to open my mouth to make some excuse, she glanced at me with a piercing, stern stare. Then, as fast as it had come, the expression was gone—replaced with a crafty twist at the corner of her lips. Her laughter broke out and echoed through the kitchen like thunder, washing away all my anxious thoughts.

"Why are you laughing?" I asked, perplexed.

Evie's laughter faded as she shook her head. "We couldn't even make it two weeks without telling anyone. And who didn't we tell? The one person who could have been legally obligated to keep the secret. Josie."

I felt my cheeks flush red with embarrassment as my

daughter pointed out the comedic incredulousness of our predicament.

Evie's face changed again, this time to one of determination. "We have to figure out what's going on here because clearly something is, and I don't want to wind up in jail," she said firmly. "Let's sit down at the table and go over what we know so far."

I nodded solemnly in agreement.

We knew Beau was killed, and his body dumped—but we didn't know how he was killed, or with what. We knew Fiona was killed with a gun in town when she was supposed to be in jail. We knew a gun—possibly the same gun—wound up on shelter property, and that it had been found by the son of the crooked mayor.

And finally, Jessa Winthrop's demand for Belladonna to be given to her now seemed even more suspicious, as if she already knew what the will would say before it was opened.

"Do you know anything else, Mom?" Evie asked, tapping information on a tablet. "Maybe something that seemed innocent? Something Fiona said? Something you heard in town? Anything, really."

I shook my head and looked around the room—and that's when I spotted it. On the floor in the kitchen corner was a bag from Garcia's Corner Market. "You know, now that you mention it, I saw Cecelia Goddard at Garcia's the other day. She mentioned she hoped the police would finish with Wardwell Manor sooner rather than later because she was due a commission on it."

Evie stopped typing and looked up at me with wide eyes. "Mom?" she asked in disbelief. "Are you serious?"

I nodded. "That's what she said."

"You don't need a real estate agent unless you're going to buy or sell a property. Why would she think she was going to sell that house and get a commission off it before the will was even read?"

"It's not necessarily suspicious. Maybe she just hoped she'd get to sell it for whoever inherited it."

Evie cocked her head to the side, her mind considering all the possibilities. Then suddenly, as if a brilliant light had turned on in her head, a smile crossed her face. "I know! Let's call and find out how much we could get if we sold Wardwell Manor!"

"We haven't decided to sell it yet—"

"You know that. I know that. She doesn't," my daughter replied knowingly. Her voice held a hint of satisfaction.

"Okay, this place is huge," Evie said. "I can't believe we inherited this place."

"The shelter inherited this place," I corrected.

When we arrived at Wardwell Manor, Cecelia stood there, radiating southern beauty and power. Her dark hair was tied back in a tight knot, and the fake-diamond buttons on her black suit glistened in the sunlight. As she welcomed us, her red lips parted in a fake smile.

"I'm so excited that you've decided to sell this place," she said with a broad, welcoming smile.

"We haven't decided on that yet. We just need to know what the estimated salability of this property is," Evie said firmly, Darla behind her. "So we can make a decision whether or not to sell it."

"Of course, of course," said Cecilia Goddard. "Your carpenter, Landon, is out back boarding up some broken windows until he can order the replacement windows."

"Great," I said.

"Yes. You're very lucky." The real estate agent's full lips curled into a wide smile, but there was a crease in her forehead that betrayed her true feelings. She must be irritated that Landon, who I'd called, took charge of the repairs, but she was too sales-focused to criticize his presence. "I'm sure you'll want to sell as soon as possible, right? Without making major repairs?"

"No. As Evie said, we're not sure what we'll be doing with it," I told her.

"That entirely depends on what you tell us, Cecelia." Evie's exuberant answer drowned my answer out without a moment's hesitation.

"Well, Wardwell Manor has six bedrooms and seven bathrooms, so it should be plenty of room for you, all your cats, and your two girls if you decide to keep the place," Cecilia told us. "There's an upstairs and a downstairs, so you can separate living areas and shelter areas a bit more than you can now—you'll have bedrooms for both your girls."

Darla smiled. "I just work here."

Evie gently punched her shoulder. "Oh, stop. No one just works here."

"You have a few challenges with the house, however," Cecelia warned us. "There has been a lot of trouble with the plumbing and electricity, because of age and the erosion of the limestone below the house. There are a few broken pipes, the wiring could use some upgrading, and so on."

"Oh, that's not a problem," Evie assured her. "We can do that."

Could we, now?

I was pretty sure I'd never seen Evie hold a hammer in her life.

Cecelia nodded understandingly and motioned for us to follow her inside.

We passed through several rooms before coming to one with an enormous fireplace and several pieces of furniture that looked like they belonged in a museum.

"This was where Fiona spent most of her time in her later years," Cecelia explained quietly as she pointed at various items around the room. "They would be worth quite a bit if they were sold off piece by piece—but I think it would be best to keep them all together as one package deal. Since the furniture has such sentimental value."

How would Cecelia Goddard know what room Fiona lived in, much less what furniture had sentimental value?

Even as I wondered, it was clear from her tour that Cecelia had a deep understanding and appreciation for the house. She pointed out the intricate woodwork and handcrafted furnishings, as well as the original artwork still hanging on the walls. She even opened up an old chest to reveal a collection of vintage china she claimed had been in the Blackwell family for generations.

"This house is incredible," Darla breathed.

"It is incredibly unique for this area, yes."

Finally, we came to a room filled with bookshelves and bookcases, each carefully labeled and cataloged. Cecelia told us this was Fiona's personal library—a treasure trove of knowledge both inherited and accumulated over her lifetime.

We stood in awe at the sheer volume of books before us—every genre imaginable, fiction and nonfiction. I even spotted what must be rare editions displayed on pedestals.

"This room stays just like this," Evie breathed, her eyes wide.

The tour concluded at a place Cecelia claimed was Fiona's favorite spot in the back garden—an ancient stone bench veiled by verdant foliage. The area was guarded by towering trees that locked out the chaotic sounds of the outside world. I could almost see the ghost of Fiona seated there in quiet contemplation, Belladonna chasing butterflies among the flowers.

The entire property felt like it was from another era,

but it could be brought up to date with a few modern touches.

"Truthfully, Eleanor, I'd love to get the commission for this, but if I inherited this house? Honestly, I wouldn't be able to part with it." Cecelia smiled warmly. "I think this is an incredible opportunity for you all—it will require some work. But if handled properly, I believe it can become something really special again."

"How do you know so much about the house?" Evie asked. "You're practically an expert, and I thought Fiona kept to herself."

Cecelia smiled once more, her eyes twinkling knowingly. "Jessa gave me a file full of information about it. She said Fiona was planning to sign the house over to Beau and Jessa or something like that, and she wanted me to be prepared to put it on the market and answer questions I might get about its condition and history." Her smile faltered. "That was before the two of them passed, of course. Though even after, she assumed Fiona would have left the house to Beau."

"She must have been pretty surprised by that will reading," Evie said.

"Yes. She was." Cecelia nodded.

"I don't understand. Why would it matter? Beau was dead. What would have happened to the house if Fiona left it to Beau?" Darla questioned, eyebrows furrowed in bewilderment.

"Well, if Fiona hadn't gone and left that estate to your shelter, it would've gone to Beau," Cecelia said, her

Texas accent deepening as the conversation became more casual. "Beau left it all to Jessa in his will, so she was the one who would've gotten the estate—if it hadn't of been for Fiona's surprise move. She couldn't believe it —but then again, I think she should've seen it coming. Everyone knew about how Fiona was about that cat of hers." Cecelia's smile was a sad one.

Evie and I exchanged astonished looks, our eyebrows shooting up in shock.

The realization hit me like a ton of bricks. If Beau had passed, the entire estate and all of Fiona's hard work would have gone to Jackson Winthrop.

Chapter Eighteen

As we walked back toward the house, the
silence was almost oppressive. Our steps seemed to
reverberate through the air. I took in all the remnants of
Fiona's life that remained—old pictures, furniture, books
—and felt a wave of emotions wash over me.

The house seemed like more than just a building; it
was a living memory of its former occupant and her life
—and going forward, it would be a testament to her love
for cats. Cecelia was right. The place was amazing.

At the far end of the hallway, I could make out
Landon's figure. The closer we came, though, the more I
sensed something was off. I noticed Landon's face was
pinched and there were creases in his forehead. His eyes
moved back and forth between the door and me, and he
chewed on his bottom lip nervously.

"Hey, Landon," I said. "Thanks for boarding up
those windows. Do you know what happened to them?"

"Ellie," he said gruffly. His overalls were flecked with sawdust, and his carpenter's tool belt was heavy with hammers, screwdrivers, and chisels. "Let me show you what I've done as a temporary fix, and what will need to be done."

"Sure."

He gestured for me to follow him into a room on the side, already moving quickly in that direction.

"Hey, um, Mom?" Evie was practically vibrating with excitement, her hands clasped tightly together and a broad smile on her face. "Darla and I are going to go look at the library," Evie said.

Darla stood next to her, a wide grin on her face as she nodded in agreement.

"Okay, just be careful."

We stepped into the room, and a wave of warmth greeted us. Sunlight streamed in from the three windows, though one had been expertly patched with thick wood. Shelves lined the walls, and a cluttered oak desk stood in the corner next to the boarded-up window.

"This is just temporary, but it's secure," he said, running his hand over the wood next to him. "We'll need to make sure all these windows are secured properly with better glass, and I noticed we'll want to add some new insulation as well."

"Landon, this is general construction," I said to the carpenter. "You don't need to do this."

"It's the least I can do," he muttered. He cleared his throat, and his voice sharpened as he turned toward the real estate agent. "Cecelia, are you staying around here?" he asked. "There's a lot I need to go over with Ellie as far as repairs and the like. Maybe it'd be best if you came back after they were all done."

I could sense the sudden tension in the room as Landon's eyes flashed at Cecelia, and I gave an almost imperceptible nod of agreement. She seemed to take the hint, because moments later she was saying her goodbyes and reaching out to give me a hug. As she stepped out of the door, Landon released a deep breath of relief.

"What's wrong?"

"Someone broke into this place after the police were here, and they broke in to take something from that desk," he said as he pointed to the desk in the corner.

I stepped closer and noticed that one drawer had its lock broken, its contents spilled across the floor. "How do you know it was after the police were here?" I asked, my curiosity piqued.

"This was a crime scene for two days," Landon said. "They wouldn't have left a window wide open like that for anyone to crawl through. They would have boarded it up to avoid any lawsuits for damages. Besides, those papers? Look here," he said.

"Okay," I said, and moved closer.

He moved to the desk and carefully lifted an old book with a faded cover and yellowed pages from its top. "This is all handwritten," he said as he flipped through the pages. "It rained three days ago—if this was sitting on top of this desk under that broken window during a rain storm, all the writing would be smeared. But it isn't."

"Wait, let me see that."

Landon handed it to me.

The book was filled with Fiona's handwriting; her notes, musings, drawings, and stories all carefully preserved within its worn pages. It seemed that she had kept this book as some sort of personal diary or journal.

My gaze dropped to the drawer with the rusty latch, and I carefully prodded it open. Papers were shoved inside in chaotic disarray. I squinted my eyes in disbelief and shook my head. "What a mess. You're probably right, but how can we tell what's missing if we don't even know what was there to begin with?"

Landon sighed, his eyes scanning the desk. "We can't tell if anything's missing, but it's clear that someone was looking for something Fiona owned, and they were willing to break in here to get it." He ran a hand over his forehead, his expression grim. "That's new information."

I studied his features as I thoughtfully chewed on my bottom lip. "We'll just have to figure it out as we go," I said. I hoped I sounded confident.

He narrowed his eyes, brows knitted together in confusion. "And how do we do that?" he asked with a hint of skepticism in his voice.

I guess I didn't sound all that confident.

I suggested we begin by going through the papers in the desk, sorting them into related piles and noting if anything seemed to be missing. Landon watched as I worked and then, finally, jumped in to help, his hands moving deftly over each document with a speed and confidence that left me impressed.

"So, that's it?" he asked when we finished.

"Well, for the moment, that's it," I said. "Okay, so, that pile is about the house and Fiona's Blackwell inheritance. This one is all journals or notes or scribbles, informal stuff. That over there is all the legal paperwork, and that pile is all correspondence with friends and family."

We stood motionless for a few minutes, eyeing the stacks of documents. Landon ran his hands through his hair, turned to me, and said in a hushed tone, "I don't know how that helped."

I looked up, my eyes meeting his. "I don't know, but they were trying to find something specific," I said, my gaze sweeping across the papers. "This is a ton of information, and none of it was taken. We can at least get an idea of the types of information kept in this desk and figure out—" I stopped talking as my eyes fell on the overflowing trash can. "Landon, look."

An envelope rested right on top, crumpled and partially torn.

I reached over and smoothed it flat on the desk—it was addressed to Beau Blackwell and had a return address from a law office in Dallas. I looked inside. "It's empty."

He studied the envelope carefully before nodding

slowly. " Do you think this could be connected to what they were looking for?"

I hesitated, weighing the risk of telling him the truth.

"Take a seat. I have something you probably need to hear." I motioned to the chair, my gaze never wavering from him.

Landon hesitated for a moment, but did as instructed.

He fixed me with a stare, then shook his head slowly. "This is really stretching the limits of my credulity, I gotta admit," he told me.

"Look, I get it. I'm pretty clear on how ridiculous this sounds. So far, all I know is that a cat claimed there was a secret baby. I don't know that it's true." I held up the envelope. "Though this certainly makes me think Belladonna might have been right."

"Because it's from Dallas."

I nodded. "And if Jackson exists, anyone in Jessa's world would have a motive to kill Fiona even before Beau was killed. Now that we inherited, trying to blame someone at the shelter for the murder makes sense, too. I mean, that has to be why that gun was planted, right? If it's the gun that killed Fiona."

He fixed me with a piercing stare, then sighed heavily. "It's the gun that killed Fiona. I had breakfast with Mario at Dale's this morning." Mario was a friend of Landon's that worked for the Tablerock Police Department. "He wanted to apologize for acting all serious the other day, and he let me know forensics had confirmed the match to the murder. So things were a little less tense at the station."

"The murder. Just Fiona? Not Beau?"

"Beau wasn't killed with a gun. Beau was killed by —" Landon stopped and sat straight up. "Beau was killed with a carbon arrow."

"So Beau was killed...with a bow?"

Landon nodded.

I couldn't help but laugh. "This whole thing is getting more and more ridiculous."

"Not so much, though. Remember what I said that day you patched me up?"

"You'll have to be more specific. You said a lot of things that day."

"That kid I chased, the goth kid everyone was throwing rocks at? Remember, I saw him at Bowell's, perusing a rack of crossbows made of carbon, with the doctor in tow? You'd use a carbon bow in a crossbow. I think."

My jaw dropped. "Do you believe that kid sauntering around in his Gothic regalia could actually be Jackson Winthrop?"

Landon gave a noncommittal shrug. "It's far-fetched, but it's worth investigating. We should go talk to Doc Canter about it. See what he says about that day, maybe get an idea of the kid's identity."

"What if Doc's involved?" I asked suspiciously, my gaze narrowing.

"He's been living here for years, Ellie. Everyone in this town loves him."

Not everyone.

"I'd be surprised if he was involved in something like this, but it doesn't hurt to ask the right questions. Or meet in a public place," Landon said with a shrug. "I'll call him and set up drinks at Grackle Tavern and then lock this place up. You go get Evie and Darla. We can swing by the shelter and drop them off, then head out to meet Tony."

Tony arrived at the Grackle Tavern a few minutes before us. He was already seated at the bar, nursing a beer and scanning the room with a wary eye. When he saw us, he stood up and motioned toward one of the booths that lined the large room. "Landon. Ellie," he said, his voice friendly. "Can I get you two anything?"

We both nodded our heads and Tony signaled the waitress. We ordered two glasses of cold beer, a plate of nachos, and a basket of fries. We followed him over to the booth, sliding into the worn leather seats as we waited for our drinks to arrive.

The Grackle Tavern was an old-fashioned bar with dim lighting, wood paneling on the walls, and a jukebox playing classic rock music in the corner. The air was filled with the smell of fried food and stale beer.

We all settled into the booth, Tony lounging against the vinyl seat. He propped his elbows on the table and leveled a piercing glare at me. "What's so important that it can't wait?" he asked, his voice slightly edged with suspicion.

I cleared my throat and, in a careful and measured voice, I said, "We wanted to ask you about the goth kid Landon noticed when you were at Bowell's a few weeks ago. We think he was the same person everyone was pelting with rocks on the day Fiona was wounded. Can you tell us who it is? You didn't appear to know him that day, and yet Landon saw you with the kid."

Dr. Tony Canter paled.

For the first time, I suddenly felt aware that my beer booth companion, who had been vaguely familiar to me before, might be a killer, and a chill ran down my spine. He was disgusting, yes—but a murderer? My heart skipped a beat as the smell of sweat, spilled beer and cigarette smoke hung in the air over the table's silence.

After a moment, Doc Canter sat back in his chair and sighed. "Yes, I know who he is," he admitted. "A boy named Jackson Talbert. I know little about him, other than he's an orphan from the Dallas area, and he lost his Mom just six months ago to a quick bout with Cancer."

"How did you meet him?" I asked.

"He was staying at the county youth shelter I volunteer at for a while. He left suddenly a few days ago with no explanation or trace."

Jackson Talbert. It was too close, too much of a coincidence—but not proof. I wished I had Evie here so she could look up what the mayor's maiden name had been.

"You don't know anything else about him?" Landon asked.

Doc shook his head. "Not much. He was a scout for years. That's why I took him to Bowell's and then hunting on Haberman's land." Dale Haberman, the donut shop owner, had a property on the edge of town that many people in Tablerock used for hunting wild hogs and deer. "He just seemed unhappy and alone, so I tried to help him out."

Landon nodded. "Why didn't you tell the police you knew who he was that day?"

He paused for a moment, then said, "Look, I know I should have done more when I saw him that day. Maybe if I had said something or—" Tony Canter paused, his face twisted with regret. "I just didn't want to tell the police who he was, so I just pretended I didn't know him. I'm sure him breaking into JD's pickup truck was an accident. And once Fiona got shot? I definitely wasn't saying anything then."

Tony's refusal to acknowledge Jackson annoyed me. That young man, from what I saw, needed an ally on his side that day. Tony Canter decided he wouldn't be there and left him to fend for himself against the mob alone.

"JD Lance, right?" I asked. "What does he do for a living again?"

Tony took a long sip of his cold beer before setting it back on the metal coaster. He ran a hand across his mouth and cleared his throat before continuing. "Well, no one said anything, Ellie, but I heard JD's a retired lawyer. Used to practice family law back in the day."

I slowly ran my finger along the faded crease of a town newspaper someone had left in the booth and leaned in to get a better look at the picture of the mayor beneath the headline. I squinted, trying to make out the details, and then looked up from the paper to address Tony once more. "I know it's a long shot, but do you know what her maiden name was?" I asked.

"Who?"

I tapped the paper.

Doc Canter leaned in close and squinted at the discolored image. His eyes widened, and he leaned back and gasped. "It's Talbert!" Tony shook his head in disbelief and glanced between the two of us. "You think Jackson is related to the mayor? I mean, how did you even get that idea?"

I could see the realization sink in on Landon's face. We locked eyes for a moment before I continued, telling Tony that we'd heard a rumor the mysterious kid might be related to Jessa Winthrop, and also might hold the answer to who killed Fiona and what their motive had been.

Landon leaned closer, his eyes darting around

Tony's face as he spoke. "We just need to find him. Do you know where he is?"

Tony squirmed under the scrutiny, licking his lips nervously before finally asking, "Are you gonna hurt him? I mean, from what I heard, he gave you quite a wallop. I'm not gonna help you track him down just so you can exact revenge."

"No, nothing like that," Landon said firmly.

Canter's eyes narrowed as he weighed the potential risks, his jaw ticking as he deliberated.

"Come on, Tony," I said with a smile. "When have you known Landon to run around town beating up teenagers? You're the pediatrician. You'd probably know before everyone else. Jackson's a kid."

He swept his gaze over Landon's face, searching for any sign of deception before finally taking a breath and nodding. "Okay." His voice had a determined edge to it, and he leaned forward. "Let's go find him, then."

Chapter Nineteen

THE SUN WAS SINKING BELOW THE HORIZON, painting the sky in a beautiful blend of pinks and oranges as we headed out of town in search of Jackson Talbert. We had no idea where he might be, but Tony seemed to have an inkling, and he volunteered to drive.

In the backseat, I texted Evie. *In case I wind up dead, doc did it.*

LOL, she texted back.

Not kidding. L and I in doc's truck heading out of town to find J.

OMG Mom. Turn on 20 sharing right now.

I blinked. *20 what?*

Location sharing! Turn it on!

Years ago, I made Evie enable location sharing, so I could track her whereabouts. This was less about my overprotective mother and more about my desire to locate her if she ended up in a hospital. I did as she asked

—at least I think I did—and then tried to relax by looking out the window at the hill country that stretched on for miles.

Tony told us stories about his family's history in this part of Texas and commented on various landmarks we passed as we drove. He described how his great-great-grandfather was a Confederate soldier who fought in the Civil War and how his family had ranched this land for years. "I take it, though you wouldn't be impressed with that history." He paused. "Since you're a social justice warrior cat rescue person."

When I looked up, he was watching me in the rear-view mirror. "I actually find it fascinating," I said. "Everyone should be proud of their family and where they come from, even if that pride is essentially just over-coming familial adversity."

And everyone should be given the opportunity to learn about themselves, I thought, my mind on Jackson.

Tony Canter agreed with a smile and a nod before returning his attention to the road. For a few minutes, we drove in silence until he pointed out an old one-room cabin nestled in the hills. "Do you see that cabin up near the trees? My great-grandfather built that. He built that cabin with his own two hands over a century ago, and it's still standing today."

"Good for him," I said.

"Is that where you think Jackson is?" Landon asked.

"I believe so. I offered it a few times, explaining that if things got too tough at the shelter, he could bunk there.

I'm not a millionaire—far from it—but I have that cabin with running water, electricity, and a fireplace to keep him warm if the weather turns cold." In the rear-view mirror, he gave me a knowing look. "Of course you'd despise it," he said. "No air conditioning."

Okay, first, Tony Canter and I were not close enough for him to make as many assumptions as he did on this car ride. Second? The sleazy womanizer was awfully generous where this kid was concerned.

Tony exited the main road and took a dirt path up the hill until we reached a clearing in the trees. In the center of it, his cabin stood starkly against the shadowed grove. The old wood structure had a rusty metal roof, and it was surrounded by a tall fence made of discarded pallets and old wooden boards.

The car stopped momentarily when Tony spotted a cruiser parked in front of the cabin. It was adorned with the classic logo of the Tablerock Police Department. It stood out sharply against the rustic surroundings, its bright paint contrasting with the shadows of the grove.

Landon and Tony both stiffened, exchanging uneasy glances as we pulled up beside the cruiser. Before either of them could speak, a tall, broad-shouldered officer emerged from the cabin. His penetrating gaze and his authoritative stance made it clear that he was in charge.

We got out of the car.

"You must be Doc Canter," he said gruffly, not even sparing Landon and me a glance before walking over to shake Tony's hand. "I'm Officer Winthrop with the Tablerock Police Department. Jackson's told me about the help you've offered him."

Officer Winthrop.

Officer Joel Winthrop.

Jessa Winthrop's son.

Jackson Talbert's half brother.

I saw a figure in the cabin's doorway, a young man wearing a black leather jacket with silver studs and a spiky mohawk. His posture was unsteady, and his eyes shifted around the clearing as if he expected something to jump out at him. "Joel?" he asked, his voice barely above a whisper. "What's going on?"

"Go back inside, Jackson. I'll take care of this."

"But—"

"I said go inside."

Jackson complied.

Officer Winthrop turned to us, his voice professional. "Doc Canter, I'm sorry for the trouble. Jackson's been living here for the past couple of weeks, with your permission?" The question was more a statement than an inquiry.

Tony nodded. "So it would seem."

Officer Winthrop nodded back. "Well, it looks like we have a situation on our hands here. I don't want to cause any unnecessary problems between you, so I think it might be best if Jackson comes back with me and stays at my place until this whole thing blows over—"

Until what thing blows over?

"Stay at your place? Who are you to him?" I asked, blurting it out without thinking.

My voice had barely left my lips when Landon rushed to my side. His stance was powerful, commanding, and I swore I could feel the energy radiating off him like electricity. He watched the officer with hawk-like intensity, and I knew he would rain down destruction if anyone dared to step in my direction.

Which, let's be honest, I might need.

Considering the way my mouth started moving without thinking and all.

Winthrop's eyes narrowed, and he planted his feet, brazenly drawing himself to his full height. His arms were folded across his chest and one eyebrow was slightly raised in a challenging arch. His voice was cool and measured when he asked, "I beg your pardon, ma'am?"

"Well, this is unincorporated land, not Tablerock proper," I pointed out. "And it's Doc Canter's private land on top of that. So that's two reasons you shouldn't be here."

"Is that so?" he said in a low, menacing tone.

"Yep. That's so. Which is why I wonder who that young man is to you." I tried to keep my voice light but authoritative, a tone I had perfected after years of practice as a mom.

Winthrop's face hardened, and his gaze turned cold. "Jackson is my brother," he said gruffly. He stepped closer, towering over me with a fierce intensity that sent a chill down my spine. "Now, if you don't mind, I think it's time for us to be on our way. We can discuss this further at the station."

Landon's body went rigid while all the breath seemed to rush out of me as Winthrop's voice triggered a forgotten memory. Every muscle in my body clenched as if I'd been struck by lightning.

"What is it?" Landon asked me.

"The morning Fiona was arrested," I said, my voice shaking slightly. "Two days before she was shot—he was at my property. I talked to him through the intercom."

Winthrop's face hardened as a muscle twitched in his jaw. He narrowed his eyes and gritted his teeth. He spoke through gritted teeth, "You have a remarkable memory for someone of your years."

"Hey," Landon said sharply. "Watch it."

"Why would you have been there?" I asked no one in particular. "You couldn't have been dumping the gun —or finding it. It was before Fiona got shot." I raced through all the mental facts we'd stumbled over, all the behaviors, all the suspicions. "Then why were you there? And you were there twice..."

Joel didn't move a muscle as we stared each other down. In the silence, I could hear the faint sound of Jackson rummaging around inside the cabin. Or maybe that was all the disparate facts flying around in my brain whacking into each other, trying to make it all make sense.

Finally, it hit me, and I gasped.

"You were waiting for Fiona's cat," I said.

Winthrop's face flushed a deep purplish red, and I could tell I had struck a nerve. His nostrils flared, and his jaw clenched tightly, as if he was struggling to keep his anger in check. "I think it's time for you two to leave."

"I think this is my property, Joel," Doc Canter told the officer. "I don't know what the hell is going on here, but I know they were invited. So was Jackson. You weren't." The doc looked at me. "What cat? What are you talking about?"

"Property!" I blurted out. "When Cecelia said Tablerock PD was at Wardwell Manor investigating—that was you! It couldn't have been anyone else. The county was handling the case. Not your department."

Winthrop glared at me with such unrestrained fury I almost stepped back in surprise. "You don't know what you're talking about," he said, his voice tight with anger.

"What were you looking for?" I asked. "Beau's will?"

Jackson poked his head through the door, his face full of worry. "Joel," he called out, "are you coming back in?"

When Joel heard his brother's voice, he lost control of his temper.

The officer whirled around, pointing an accusing finger at Jackson. Spit flew from his mouth as he shouted,

"What the heck do you think we're doing out here? Didn't I tell you to stay inside? Do you have no common sense? A mutt could follow orders better than you, you imbecile!" His face flushed a deep crimson, and his fists were so tightly balled that his knuckles whitened. Taking a ragged breath and glancing away, he finished in a low voice, "Never mind. Just get back in the house. Now."

Jackson cringed and stepped back as Joel's face twisted in anger.

"You knew," I said quietly, Joel's disdain for his younger brother bringing what happened into sharp focus. "You knew about your half brother sent off to live with your aunt in Dallas. You knew he was Beau's son. And you knew that Fiona's will left all the money with whoever cared for the cat." I glanced at Jackson, who still looked frightened by his older brother's fury. "You used your younger brother to—"

"Shut up," he warned.

"And who else but a cop could get Fiona out of jail? I can't believe I missed it. You crafted a plan that would ensure your half brother's inheritance, while also punishing Fiona for her supposed wrongdoings." I blinked. "But no...you hate Jackson. It's clear—"

"Ellie, maybe we should just go," Landon said quietly.

Joel stepped forward, his face contorted in rage. "You think I killed them?" he snarled. "You think I would do something like that?"

His tone was so menacing, my heart started pounding in my chest.

"Joel, she didn't say that," Doc Canter told him.

"I didn't, but I should have," I blathered on like I was wearing a bulletproof girdle. "Obviously, he killed Fiona thinking the inheritance would ricochet back to him through his brother." I glanced toward the cabin. "Thing is, he obviously can't stand his brother, so how was that going to work? Kill him, too?"

"Ellie?" Landon whispered.

"Yes?"

"Be quiet."

Joel Winthrop's eyes narrowed and a single bead of sweat ran down his forehead as his hand darted to his holster. His fingers fumbled, then found their grip. He pulled out a black revolver, the barrel glinting in the faint moonlight. Without hesitation, he cocked the gun— a sharp click cutting through the quiet night air—and pointed it directly at me.

Well.

Crap.

"Or I could be wrong. I mean, it's just a guess." I joked, attempting to remain calm despite the intense fear I felt. My heart felt like a caged beast, beating wildly against my rib cage. My vision narrowed until all I could see was Joel's angry face, his gun pointed at me.

He was ready to shoot.

I could feel it.

Tony Canter stood in front of the angry police officer, hands trembling in his pockets. "It's me, Doc Canter. We've known each other since you were a young boy. You're not a killer; you're a good man." He spoke softly, yet every word rang with conviction.

But he is a killer, though, I thought to myself. Possibly twice over.

Who am I kidding?

Probably twice over.

"Doc," Joel said through gritted teeth. "Stay out of it."

The doctor's face wore a look of concern as he stepped closer to Joel and placed a comforting hand on his shoulder. Meanwhile, Landon moved closer almost hovering protectively. His face was tense, but his voice was soft as he asked if I was okay.

I nodded, too frightened to speak.

"You can still turn this around, Joel," Doc Canter said gently. "Put the gun down and let us all talk about what we can do here. No one has to get hurt. You have a chance at something different if you just step away from this now."

Joel's grip on the gun tightened. "No. No. It's too late."

"Nothing you've done is so bad that it can't be fixed," Canter said.

I beg to differ on that one, I thought. But I sure as hell would not open my mouth with a gun a few inches from my face.

"It's too late. He can't do this to us," Joel seethed

through gritted teeth. "All those years my mother stayed with that rich old man, and all we got was crumbs. This is our chance. Our chance to get what we're owed."

"Who, Joel?" Doc asked. "Who can't do this to you?"

Joel bellowed "Beau!" at the top of his lungs like he was feeling the humiliation and pain of childhood all over again. "You come along like you deserve something from them!" he shouted, jabbing an accusing finger in Jackson's direction. "The Blackwells caused me a lifetime of shame and heartache! I'm the one who stayed here and dealt with it all! You think you deserve the money he promised my mother? You come here expecting some kind of payback from the family that screwed my mother over time and time again?"

The gun trembled in his hand. I could feel the tension in the air, like a storm was about to break.

"And you know what? Fine. Yeah." Joel said, his voice shaking with anger. "I killed them both. I shot Beau with one of the wonder boy's arrows, so he'd get blamed and then be gone. But then I realized Fiona would have left her fortune to Beau, right? So if I shot her, too, he'd get it all—and then once he was gone, I'd get it all. Finally! So I shot Fiona after my girlfriend got her out of jail."

Doc Carter looked heartbroken. "Joel, how could you?"

"It had to be done; they would never have given us what we deserved if they had lived."

"You and Jackson?" he asked, confused.

"No, idiot, me and my mother. Now it's my turn to get what I deserve, and no one is going to stand in my way! Not any of you, and especially not some cat rescue!" He was shaking now, and I could see the hatred in his eyes. He tightened his grip on the gun, steeling himself for what he was about to do.

As a deafening silence settled over us, my thoughts raced. I realized he would kill me.

No one breathed.

"Mom!" A tinny, faint voice came out of my pocket. My heart skipped a beat, and I was suddenly aware that my hand was still in that same pocket, gripping the phone tightly. "Mom! Answer me!"

My pulse raced some more, and my breath caught as Joel's gaze snapped to me, his gun steady in his hand. His eyes widened in surprise as he slowly scanned the clearing, searching for the source of the voice.

Then the soft sound of sirens.

"I got everything he said recorded! Mom! Mom! Tell him the sheriff is on his way over to Doc's cabin! With tons of cops! Everyone knows! Mom!" Even though her voice was faint, I could tell Evie was screaming at the top of her lungs. "When you turned on the location thing, you called me! Darla and I heard everything! We've been listening the whole time! We recorded it all! Mom! Mom, are you okay? Mom!"

The sound of the sirens seemed to get closer, and the air felt electric with tension.

Joel's hands shook and the gun he had held clattered

to the ground. He stared intently at Jackson for a moment before turning back to us, his expression a mixture of defeat and despair.

Quick as a flash, Landon lunged for the gun. He wrapped his finger around the trigger, pointing it directly at Officer Joel Winthrop as the blue and red strobes of the approaching cavalry lit up his face, and he closed his eyes.

"Fine. It's over. I don't want to hurt anyone else. I just wanted what was mine. I know that doesn't make it right." Joel clenched his jaw and balled his hands into fists as the sirens grew louder and closer. Just then, he opened his eyes. "My mother had nothing to do with this. Remember that. I did this for her, not with her."

The sheriff's cruiser squealed to a stop, followed by two more. Nearly a dozen deputies spilled out, guns already in hand and shouts of orders filling the air. Joel was surrounded, his hands raised in submission. His face was expressionless as the handcuffs clicked in place and the officers led him away.

We all watched in shocked silence as he was led away.

"We got a confession from Joel's girlfriend late this afternoon—her fingerprints were found on one bullet in the gun," Deputy Markham told us as we waited for the sheriff to finish processing the scene. "She said Joel was desperate. Resentful of his surprise brother, wanting what he thought he deserved and Jackson didn't. His simmering resentment boiled over into an act of revenge against Beau and Fiona."

"But how did he know about Jackson being back in town at all?" I asked.

"Leila Tucker—his girlfriend."

My mind raced. Wasn't she the woman working at the county jail? I had seen the woman in the visitation room, the one talking on her phone. "She works at the county jail." I said. "I saw her in the room when I went to visit Fiona."

The deputy nodded gravely. "Leila was the one that helped Joel break Fiona out of jail. She was waiting for Joel over at Mayor Winthrop's one night when Beau showed up with papers from a Dallas lawyer, furious that Jackson was suing him for back support payments. With his guardian deceased, Jackson held control of her estate, and he could sue his legal father for all the support he never gave. Jessa never formally allowed Jackson to be adopted by her sister."

"I wonder why not," Landon said.

I waved the question away. "Is that when Joel learned of Jackson's existence?"

Markham nodded at me. "Leila told Joel what she heard, and it apparently made Joel snap. His anger and need for revenge snowballed into a plot. He wanted to get rid of the Blackwells and his brother, so he could take the estate. What he didn't count was Fiona changing her will and leaving everything to a cat rescue." Don Markham looked at me. "Jackson may still challenge Fiona's will, by the way. Since he's Beau's child."

I looked over at Jackson Talbert. He was sitting on the front steps about ten feet away, his eyes red rimmed and still filled with disbelief. "I'm sure we can work something out. After what that kid's been through, I think he deserves it all."

Jackson rose from the stairs and stepped away from the porch toward us. His voice cracked as he spoke. "I don't want it. The estate—it doesn't belong to me. I just wanted what my Mom was entitled to."

"Jackson, he was your father—"

"No," he said sharply. "He wasn't."

The sheriff arrived just then. He readjusted his gun belt and badge as he made his way up the path. "Markham," he nodded.

"Sheriff Dixon." Markham nodded back.

"I wanted to let you all know we've processed the scene, and Joel Winthrop's going to jail. I can't promise it, but my bet is he'll be held without bail."

"Good," Landon said.

"We'll need you all to come in for formal statements tomorrow," he said, turning to me. "But I wanted to let you know that thanks to your daughter, we have his entire confession on tape. Joel won't be bothering anyone again for a very long time."

"What a terrible waste," Doc Canter murmured.

"True that," Dixon nodded. "Now if you'll excuse

me, I have to go inform the mayor of Tablerock that her son's been arrested."

Markham looked relieved as the sheriff walked away.

I thought about the years of deception that had woven around him. The walls the Winthrops and the Blackwells had built, all meant to protect wealth that, in the end, went to a bunch of cats.

"Come on," Landon whispered. "Don Markham is taking Canter back to town, and Doc said I could borrow his car. Let me take you home."

Chapter Twenty

We drove back in an eerie silence, the headlights of the car illuminating the winding road ahead. I looked up at the stars, twinkling brightly against the ink-black sky like tiny pinpricks of hope as we passed the few cars out on the country road. I couldn't help but think about the events of the day.

"What do you think will happen to Jackson?" I asked Landon, breaking the quietness.

"I'm not sure. The police might get him for obstruction of justice or something, since he ran from them," he replied, his voice thoughtful. "I'm not going to press charges for the fight, though. That kid sounds like he's been through enough. And," Landon said, chuckling, "even though he looks like a deranged rooster, I get the sense that the kid is all right. A good egg."

The darkness was overwhelming, and my head was

swirling with a jumble of feelings as we drove up to the shelter. This was my entire world—it had been my home, and my ambition for five years—but now everything felt strange. This modest property held so much love and affection and many aspirations I never expected to realize.

It would be difficult to go.

Evie raced down the path, her feet pounding the ground and her hair streaming behind her. She leaped into my arms and I enveloped her in a tight hug, feeling a wave of relief wash over me. I murmured words of reassurance. "It's all right," I whispered softly. "Everything's all right."

"Are you really okay?" she asked, her voice barely above a whisper.

I nodded, a smile crossing my lips even as my eyes watered. The memory of Joel pointing a gun at me was fading with each hug from Evie and each second I spent with her. "There were a few seconds I thought I wouldn't make it out alive," I admitted, my voice trembling. "I don't know what you heard, but it was terrifying looking into his eyes while he was in such a rage."

Landon fixed me with a look, then blew out a breath and shook his head. "I'm not sure whether to be impressed by your bravery or worried about that big mouth of yours," he murmured with a smirk.

Evie laughed, her voice like bells ringing in the air. "Mom knew you were there to protect her," she said.

Landon shrugged, though a hint of a smile played on his lips. "Someone had to," he said gruffly. "That woman seems to go out of her way to stick her foot right in the center of it."

We stepped into the house.

"I didn't set out to solve a murder, I swear," I said, feeling the need to explain myself. "But when we started uncovering piece after piece of the puzzle, it felt like we had to understand what was going on. If for no other reason than Belladonna's our responsibility."

"You didn't solve a murder," Landon said. "You investigated around it and then dragged us into a confrontation with the murderer. And then, without considering the consequences, you chatted up the only suspect armed with a gun." His gaze fell on me. "On the next one, could we work harder on clues before randomly engaging with potential killers? Just a thought."

"There won't be a next time," I replied.

"Wait." Evie stepped forward, her expression full of enthusiasm. "What if there is? What if we use the crystal table thing to help the police solve crimes?"

I glared down at Evie. "Are you insane? We almost got ourselves killed this time! There was a gun pointed at me!"

Landon's eyes went wide. "Hold up, what?"

Darla clapped her hands. "We'd be great at this!"

But Evie stayed adamant. "We helped the police solve a crime no one else could—"

"No, we didn't," I cut in. "Joel's girlfriend left a fingerprint on the bullet they planted over here. We had nothing to do with it."

"No one knew about Jackson Talbert except Belladonna!"

"Not true," I argued. "Doc Center knew about him too."

"He didn't know Jackson was Jessa's kid," Landon pointed out. "And even if he did, Canter doesn't strike me as the type to get involved when he doesn't have to."

"So whose side are you on?" I asked.

Landon shrugged.

"Doc was like a big brother to Jackson at the shelter, though."

Evie held up her hands defensively. "Look, think about it—we could do so much good with this! We could use the crystal thing to help cats that come into the shelter, but when we get a cat from the police that may have witnessed a crime, we can help the police solve cases more quickly—and maybe even save lives."

"We don't even know if it works with other cats, Evie."

"Yes, we do," Darla volunteered.

"Mom, come on—we do something no one else can. It'll be a great way to contribute to our community. Suppose there's a stray with information about an unknown crime. Are we just going to ignore it? With you and Landon's old-fashioned expertise—"

"Old-fashioned?" I raised my eyebrow.

"—and me, Darla, and Matt's computer and internet research savvy—ooh! And Josie's a lawyer, so she could advise us." Evie beamed with enthusiasm, her hands wildly gesturing as she listed the many ways our friends could help. "And Laurie can be our medical expert!"

"She's a vet, Evie!"

"I'm sure something in her knowledge translates, right?"

"I would think," Darla agreed. "I mean, a wound is a wound."

Evie's enthusiasm was infectious. I couldn't help but let myself smile at the thought, even though I knew what she was proposing could be dangerous.

Dangerous, I thought, but unlikely to happen again.

Landon pondered her words for a long moment before finally responding. "I guess it could work," he said hesitantly. "We've all got the resources and knowledge to do this...but we'll need to plan and be very disciplined and"—he looked at me—"cautious."

"Why did you look at me when you said that?" I asked.

He locked eyes with me. "No reason at all, Ellie."

"What did we just do?" Landon asked me, his voice full of questions, as we stepped out onto the porch.

"Honestly? Probably nothing. The police department rarely sends cats my way—normally I'm just called to pick up strays or help with a missing pet."

"You were just humoring her?"

I shrugged. "Evie's dream is inspiring her, and I don't have the courage to tell her it won't happen." I paused and gazed up at the night sky. "I don't really want it to happen. I'm glad this is all over. It could've been much worse."

"What we did today—that was insane. I mean, you had a gun pointed at you! When I saw that, I was scared out of my mind. I almost dove at the guy! Do you know how terrified I was for you?"

I nodded slowly, recalling the fear that had filled me earlier in the evening. "Yeah. I know. That could've been terrible."

He moved closer, and I felt his warmth as he put a hand on my shoulder. "Ellie, I'm so glad you're okay. You know that, right?"

"Well," I laughed, "hopefully you are. I'd hate to think you were rooting for the killer." I turned and faced him.

He wasn't laughing.

Landon gazed into my eyes, his feelings radiating off him like a beacon. He reached out and intertwined his fingers with mine.

I tugged my hand away gently. "Landon..."

"Ellie, I know you don't share my feelings, but I still care deeply for you and can't help but be concerned about your well-being."

A small smile tugged at my lips, and I gave his hand a reassuring squeeze. "Thank you, I really appreciate it."

Finally, I released his hand.

He reluctantly let me.

Landon looked at me, searching for something.

"What is it?" I asked.

He hesitated before asking, "Do you care about me in that way at all?"

Oh, jeez.

Was it too late to choose to be shot?

"I told you," I said. "It's not about emotion. It's about Evie. She'll always live with me, always depend on me. I can't bring a man into that. She's too fragile."

"Fragile?" Landon chuckled. "That girl back there, the one who signed us up to be crime detectives based on the word of a magical cat? The one who recorded a killer's confession through a butt-dial and called the law?"

I stared at him.

"That fragile flower?" Landon laughed, admiration in his eyes. "No, Ellie. That's brave. Given the circumstances, if Evie hadn't been there to help us, I'd rather not think about what would have happened."

"That cat isn't magical," I told him. "The plate is."

"Okay, Ms. Let-me-split-that-hair. Is that all you got to say?"

I smiled. "She did good today."

"She did. I don't think you should worry about her so much—she can take care of herself. But I think you should worry about yourself a bit more—you deserve to be safe, too."

My face flushed. "Look, Landon, I like you. I really do. But I can't take the risk. Evie needs me more than anything else in the world, so dating is out of the question. That's not negotiable."

Landon nodded slowly. A silent pause hung in the air before he murmured, "Okay, Ellie. If ever you need help or a listening ear, I'm here for you. With no strings attached. But, I have to say, maybe she isn't as delicate as you think. She may be strong enough to cope with a man's entrance to your life as a helping hand. You'll never know until you give it a go."

I avoided his gaze, trying to find the strength to believe him. It was hard for Evie to trust people, and I didn't want to do anything that could hurt her emotionally.

But maybe—just maybe—he was right.

Then again, maybe I was in a weakened state after having a gun pointed at my head and I shouldn't be having this conversation right now.

"You're asking too much of me right now. With everything going on in our lives, I just don't think it's possible for me to even consider dating—not until things settle down a bit. I need to deal with the inheritance, I need to plan the move into the mansion, I have to get it ready for dozens of cats—"

"I hear you, Ellie." Landon ran a hand through his hair and smiled, his eyes crinkling. "You got it," he said, stepping back and gesturing to the room. "So, when do we start?"

Slumping into bed, I ran a hand over my face as my swirling thoughts of Landon and his words filled my mind. I wanted to believe him and yet...

It was all so complicated.

As if sensing my unrest, a warm, furry body curled up against me. My eyes went to the shadowed form of Belladonna, her soft purring like a balm to my soul. She looked up at me with her enormous amber eyes and I smiled, running my fingers through her soft fur. Sighing in contentment, I snuggled down into bed with her by my side.

"I don't know if you can understand me, Belladonna," I whispered. "But the man who killed Fiona is locked away, and we cleared her name. She didn't kill Beau."

Belladonna meowed softly and nudged me.

At that moment, everything seemed peaceful. Belladonna seemed content with her new home, and Evie and I were safe for now—even if we were in an unfamiliar situation by taking on the responsibility of the inheritance.

Landon's words echoed in my head again: "Maybe she's not as fragile as you think...maybe she's strong enough to handle the idea of a man coming into your life and helping you out. You never know until you try."

"I don't want to try," I said out loud.

Belladonna curled up against me, her gentle purring lulling me toward a peaceful sleep. I thought of Landon, and how he had been so encouraging... Maybe he was on to something—perhaps taking a risk on love again at my age wasn't as frightening as it seemed.

As if a stone had been cast in still waters, an unsettling thought rose to the surface, jolting me back to wakefulness and my eyes snapped open.

Belladonna meowed.

"Mayor Winthrop came here to find you." I squinted, trying to pick out the silhouette of the cat in the complete darkness. "Does that mean she knew about Joel's plan? How was it possible that she hadn't noticed Jackson was back in town—"?

Before I could complete my thought, I felt a gentle paw against my lips. The cat was attempting to hush me.

"You're right. I can think about all this tomorrow."

I held Belladonna close, inhaling her sweet blossom fragrance. Hesitantly, she snuggled up against me, her gentle purring rumbling through her chest. I felt her heartbeat, slow and steady.

"Goodnight, Bella."

I got a soft meow.

With every breath I took, my apprehension slowly melted away, and I drifted into a deep sleep.

Thank you for reading! I hope you enjoyed the first book in the Silver Circle Cat Rescue Mysteries!

"Honey, Hairballs, and Murder" is the next book in the series. Follow Ellie, Evie and the gang as they move into Wardwell Manor—and get into a sticky situation when a local beekeeper is murdered.

KEEP UP WITH LEANNE LEEDS

Thanks so much for reading! I hope you liked it! Want to keep up with me?

Visit leanneleeds.com to:

Find all my books...

Sign up for my newsletter...

Like me on Facebook...

Follow me on Twitter...

Follow me on Instagram...

Thanks again for reading!

Leanne Leeds

Find a typo? Let us know!

Typos happen. It's sad, but true.

Though we go over the manuscript multiple times, have editors, have beta readers, and advance readers it's inevitable that determined typos and mistakes sometimes find their way into a published book.

Did you find one? If you did, think about reporting it on leanneleeds.com so we can get it corrected.

Made in the USA
Middletown, DE
01 May 2023

29806705R00161